"Send her in."

Nothing Jaxon had read in the file prepared him for the beautiful woman who stepped inside. Avery Tierney had been a skinny, homely looking kid with scraggly, dirty brown hair and freckles, wearing hand-me-downs. She'd looked lost, alone and frightened.

This Avery was petite with chocolate-brown eyes that would melt a man's heart and curves that twisted his gut into a knot.

Although fear still lingered in those eyes. The kind of fear that made a man want to drag her in his arms and promise her everything would be all right.

"You have to help me stop the execution and get my brother released from prison," Avery said, her voice urgent.

"Why would I do that, Miss Tierney?"

A pained sound ripped from Avery Tierney's throat. "Because he's innocent."

COLD CASE IN CHEROKEE CROSSING

—

RITA HERRON

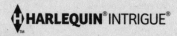

To my beautiful daughters who, as counselors,
are the real heroes.

Love you, Mom

ISBN-13: 978-0-373-69802-8

Cold Case in Cherokee Crossing

Copyright © 2014 by Rita B. Herron

Recycling programs
for this product may
not exist in your area.

Printed in U.S.A.

www.Harlequin.com

ABOUT THE AUTHOR

Award-winning author Rita Herron wrote her first book when she was twelve, but didn't think real people grew up to be writers. Now she writes so she doesn't have to get a *real* job. A former kindergarten teacher and workshop leader, she traded storytelling to kids for writing romance, and now she writes romantic comedies and romantic suspense. She lives in Georgia with her own romance hero and three kids. She loves to hear from readers, so please write her at PO Box 921225, Norcross, GA 30092-1225, or visit her website, www.ritaherron.com.

Books by Rita Herron

HARLEQUIN INTRIGUE

CAST OF CHARACTERS

Sergeant Jaxon Ward—He's supposed to make sure Hank Tierney's execution is on track—but once he meets Hank's sister, Avery, he wants to prove Hank's innocence.

Avery Tierney—She testified against her brother years ago for the murder of her foster father, Wade Mulligan. Now she must save him from death row.

Hank Tierney—He's spent his life in prison for murder. But now he claims he's innocent.

Roth Tierney—Avery and Hank's father was incarcerated for murder. Did he try to save his children by killing Wade Mulligan?

Joleen Mulligan—Wade's wife was scared of her husband. Did she kill him out of fear?

Director Landers—He worked the case when Hank was arrested. Is he hiding something?

DA William Snyderman—He was the ADA during Hank's trial. Does he know more than he's telling?

Erma Brant and Delia Hanover—The social workers who worked with the Mulligans. Did either of them know that Wade Mulligan was abusive?

Shane Fowler, Lois Thacker, BJ & Imogene Wilson—Other foster children who were abused by the Mulligans. Did one of them kill Wade and let Hank take the fall?

Prologue

Blood splattered the wood floor and walls. So much blood.

A scream lodged in nine-year-old Avery Tierney's throat. Her foster father, Wade Mulligan, lay on the floor. Limp. Helpless. Bleeding.

His eyes were bulging. The whites milky looking. His lips blue. His shirt torn from dozens of knife wounds.

The room was cold. The wind whistled through the old house like a ghost. Windowpanes rattled. The floor squeaked.

Horror made her shake all over.

Then relief.

That mean old bully could never hurt her again. Never come into her bedroom. Never whisper vile things in her ear.

Never make her do *those* things….

A noise sounded. She dragged her eyes from the bloody mess, then looked up. Her brother, Hank, stood beside the body.

A knife in his hand.

He grunted, raised the knife and stabbed Wade again. Wade's body jerked. Hank did it again. Over and over.

Blood dripped from the handle and blade. More soaked his shirt. His hands were covered….

His eyes looked wild. Excited. Full of rage.

She opened her mouth to scream again, but Hank lifted his finger to his lips and whispered, "Shh."

Avery nodded, although she thought she might get sick. She wanted him to stop.

She wanted him to stab Wade again. To make sure he was dead.

A siren wailed outside. Blue lights suddenly twirled, shining through the front window.

Hank jerked his head around, eyes flashing with fear.

Then the door crashed open and two policemen stormed in.

Hank dropped the knife to the floor with a clatter and tried to run. The bigger cop caught him around the waist.

"Let me go! Stop it!" Hank bellowed.

The skinny cop moved toward her. Then he knelt and felt Wade's neck. A second later, he looked at his partner and shook his head. "Dead."

The cop turned to her with a frown. "What happened?"

"Don't say anything!" Hank yelled.

Avery's cry caught in her throat. She didn't know what to do. What to say. She'd seen the knife in Hank's hand. Seen him stabbing Wade over and over.

Something niggled at the back of her mind. Something that had happened. Wade had come into her room…. She'd heard a noise….

"Where's your mother?" the policeman asked.

She didn't know that, either. The foster homes had been her life.

"Stop fighting me, kid." The big cop shoved Hank up against the wall, pushed his knee in Hank's back, then jerked his arms behind him.

Tears blurred Avery's eyes as he handcuffed her brother.

"It'll be okay, sis," Hank shouted.

Avery let out a sob. Hank was all she had.

What were they going to do to him? Would they take him to jail?

If they did, what would happen to her?

Chapter One

Twenty years later

"Thirty-four-year-old Hank Tierney is scheduled for execution in just a few days. Protestors against the death penalty have begun to rally, but due to Tierney's confession, his appeals have been denied."

Avery stared at the local television news in Cherokee Crossing, her heart in her throat as images from the past assaulted her.

Hank holding the bloody knife, Hank repeatedly stabbing Wade Mulligan...

Her doing nothing... She'd been in shock. Traumatized, the therapist had said. Dr. Weingarten had tried to protect her from the press. Had sat with her during the grueling forensic police interviews. Had tried to get her placed in a safe, stable home.

But nobody wanted Hank Tierney's sister.

Especially knowing their father was also in prison for murder.

That fact had worked against Hank. The assistant D.A. at the time had argued that Hank was genetically predisposed to violence. The altercations between him and their foster parents hadn't helped his case.

A couple of the neighbors had witnessed Hank lashing out at Wade when Wade had reprimanded him.

Wade's wife, Joleen, their foster mother at the time, had testified that Hank was troubled, angry, rebellious, even mean. That she'd been afraid of him for months.

Avery had been too confused to stand up for him.

But she'd secretly been relieved that Wade was dead.

And too ashamed of what the man had done to her to speak out.

"Hank Tierney was only fourteen at the time he stabbed Wade Mulligan. But due to the maliciousness of the crime, he was tried as an adult and has spent the past twenty years on death row. His sister, Avery, who was nine when the murder occurred and the sole witness of the crime, has refused interviews."

The nightmares that had been haunting Avery made her shiver. Hank's arrest and the publicity surrounding it had dogged her all her life, affecting every relationship she'd ever had.

Just as Wade's abuse had.

She was shy around men, reluctant to trust. Cautious about letting anyone in her life because once they heard her story, they usually ran.

A photo of Hank at fourteen, the day of the arrest, flashed on the screen, then a photo of him now. He was thirty-four. Not a teenager but a man.

His once thin, freckled face had filled out; his nose was crooked as if it had been broken. And he'd beefed up, added muscles to his lanky frame.

There were scars on his face that hadn't been there before, a long jagged one along his temple. But the scars in his eyes were the ones that made her lungs strain for air.

Still, he was that young boy who'd stepped in front of her and taken blows for her when Wade was drinking. Who'd sneaked her food when Wade was on one of his rampages and she was hiding in the shed out back to escape his wrath.

Hank had spent his life in jail for what he'd done. For taking away the monster who'd made her young life hell.

She should have told.

Although the therapist had assured her it wouldn't have mattered, that the number of stab wounds alone indicated Hank suffered from extreme rage and was a danger to society.

But Hank had killed Wade in self-defense. And Wade had deserved to die.

Still, her brother would be put to death in just a few days. It wasn't fair.

She looked outside the window at the dusty road and woods. The prison was only an hour from Cherokee Crossing. Subconsciously she must have chosen to settle back here because she'd be close to Hank.

Or maybe because she'd needed to confront her demons so she could move on.

Just like she had to see Hank before he died and thank him for saving her life.

TEXAS RANGER JAXON WARD took a seat in the office of Director Landers, his nerves on edge. He'd just gotten off a case and his adrenaline was still running high. Beating the suspect the way he had done could get him kicked off the job.

Hell, he didn't care.

He was ready to hang up his badge anyway. Maybe open his own P.I. agency. Then he wouldn't have to play by the rules.

"You asked to see me?"

"Yes, I've decided to grant your request to work the domestic-violence team."

Jaxon tried not to react. The director knew his background, that he'd grown up in the system and that domestic violence was personal for him.

In fact, it had been a strike against him. The director had expressed concerns that Jaxon might allow his own experiences, and his anger, to cloud his judgment, and that he'd end up taking his personal feelings out on the alleged abusers.

The director had good reason to worry.

Today was the perfect example. When he'd seen Horace Mumford go after his kid with a wood board, Jaxon had taken the board to him.

"Thank you, sir." Jaxon stood, waiting on the reprimand.

But it never came. Instead the director cleared his throat. "Your first assignment is to make sure the Tierney execution goes forward."

Jaxon frowned. "I didn't realize there was a problem."

Director Landers ran a hand over his balding head. "Some young do-gooder attorney wanting to make a name for herself is trying to get a stay and a retrial."

Jaxon had seen the recent protests against the execution in the news. Not unusual with death row cases.

"Go talk to Tierney. Make sure everything stays on track."

Jaxon's gut tightened with an uneasy feeling. "Why the interest?" According to the news, the guy was only a teenager when he murdered his foster father. And he'd been railroaded into a confession.

"Because that case was one of the first ones I worked when I was a young cop. It built my career."

Now Jaxon understood. The director was worried about his damn job, not whether or not a man was innocent.

"Wipe that scowl off your face. I didn't screw up. Hank Tierney was as guilty as his father was of murder," Director Landers said. "The kid was caught with the bloody knife in hand, blood splattered all over him. Hell, even his sister said he stabbed Mulligan."

"Fine. I'll go talk to him myself." He'd also ask about his motive. He didn't remember that being reported, only that the police thought the kid was violent and dangerous.

Director Landers gave him a warning look. "Listen, Ward, I know your history, so don't go making this kid out to be some hero or I'll can your ass. Your job is to make sure that case does not go back for a retrial. If it does, it could affect all the cases I worked after that."

That would be a nightmare.

Still, Jaxon silently cursed as he walked out of the office. Was this some kind of test to see if he followed orders?

Or did Landers just want to make sure nothing happened to tarnish his reputation?

AVERY SHIVERED AT the stark gray walls of the prison as the guard led her to a private visitors' room. Apparently the warden had arranged for them to actually be in the room together versus being divided by a Plexiglas wall.

Because she was saying a final goodbye to her brother.

She twisted her hands together as she sank into the metal chair, guilt making her stomach cramp.

She should have visited Hank before now. Should have come and thanked him for that night. Should have made sure he was all right.

The door closed, locking her in the room, and her vision blurred. Suddenly she was back there in that cold room at the Mulligan house. Lying in the metal bed with the ratty blanket…

Joleen was gone. She'd left earlier that day to take care of her mama. Avery knew it was going to be a bad night. Wade had started with the booze as soon as he'd come home from his job at the garage.

She clutched the covers and stared at the spider spinning a web on the windowpane. Rain pounded on the tin roof. Wind whistled through the eaves, rattling the glass.

"Get in there, boy."

"Don't tie me up tonight," Hank shouted. "And leave Avery alone."

Avery fought a scream. She wanted to lock the door, but she'd done that before, and it hadn't stopped him. It only made him madder. He'd broken it down with a hatchet and threatened to kill her if she locked it again.

Something slammed against the wall. Wade punching Hank. Grunts followed. Hank was fighting Wade, but Wade would win. He always won.

Footsteps shuffled a minute later, coming closer to her room. Hank shouted Wade's name, cussing him and calling him sick names.

She bit her tongue until she tasted blood. The door screeched open.

Wade's hulking shadow filled the doorway. She could smell the sweat and beer and grease from the shop. His breathing got faster.

He started toward her, and she closed her eyes. She had to go somewhere in her mind, someplace safe where she couldn't feel him touching her.

Then everything went black....

The sound of keys jangling outside the prison door startled her back to reality. The door screeched open, a guard appeared, one hand on the arm of the man shackled and chained beside him.

Hank. God... Her heart stuttered, tears filling her eyes. She remembered him as a young boy—choppy sandy blond hair, skinny legs, eyes too hard for his age, mouth always an angry line.

But he was a man now, six feet tall with muscles. His eyes were cold and hard, his face and arms scarred from prison life. He was even angrier, too, his jaw locked, a vein pulsing in his neck.

He shuffled over to the chair, pulled it out, handcuffs

rattling as he sank into it. The guard stepped to the door, folded his arms and kept watch.

She waited on Hank to look at her, and when he did, animosity filled the air between them. He hated her for not visiting.

She hated herself.

A deep sense of grief nearly overwhelmed her, and she wanted to cry for the years they'd lost. She'd spent so much of her life struggling against the gossip people had directed toward her because of her father's arrest, and then Hank's, that she hadn't thought about how he was suffering.

For what seemed like an eternity, he simply stared at her, studying her as if she were a stranger. He shifted, restless, and guilt ate at her.

"You came," he finally said in a flat voice. "I didn't think you would."

The acceptance in his tone tore at her. Maybe he didn't blame her, but he was still hurt. "I'm sorry I didn't visit you before. I should have."

Hank shrugged as if he didn't care, his orange jumpsuit stark against his pale skin. But he did care. He'd always acted tough, but on the inside he was a softie. When she was little, he used to kiss her boo-boos to make them better.

No one had been here to soothe him the past few years, though.

"I'm so sorry, Hank. At first, there was so much happening—the Department of Children and Family Services the foster system, your trial…" And then she'd had to testify to what she'd remembered.

Her testimony had sealed his fate. "I should have lied back then, said I didn't see anything."

Another tense second passed. "You were only a kid, Avery."

"So were you."

His gaze locked with hers, the memories of the two of

them huddled together out in the rain after their mother had left them returning. *I'll take care of you,* Hank had promised.

And he did.

How had she paid him back? By abandoning him.

He cleared his throat. "I tried to find out what happened to you after I got locked up, but no one would tell me anything."

Avery twined her fingers on the table. "Nobody wanted to take me," she admitted. "I wound up in a group home."

He made a low sound of disgust in his throat. "Was it bad?"

Avery picked at her fingernails to keep from rubbing that damned scar. "Not as bad as…the Mulligans." Nothing had been as bad as living with them.

Of course, Hank might argue that prison was.

"They told me you didn't remember the details of that night." Hank lowered his head, then spoke through gritted teeth. "I'm glad. I hated what he did to you. He was a monster."

Shame washed over Avery. She'd never told anyone except the therapist the truth. But Hank knew her darkest secret.

Avery reached across the table and laid one hand on his.

"I'm so sorry for everything, Hank. I know you killed Wade for me." Tears clogged her throat. "I…should have spoken up, told someone about what he was doing. Maybe it would have helped get you off, or at least they'd have given you some leniency and a lighter sentence."

Hank studied her for a long few minutes, his expression altering between anger and confusion. "You still don't remember?"

She swallowed hard. "Just that he was drinking. That you fought with him, and he tied you up. Then he came in my room." She pressed a finger to her temple, massaging where a headache pounded. The headaches always came when she struggled to recall the details. "Then everything went black until I saw you with that knife."

Hank pulled his hand away and dropped his head into his hands. "God, I don't believe this."

Avery watched him struggle, her heart pounding.

"Hank, I'm sorry. I should have lied about seeing you with that knife. You always stood up for me, and I let you down." Her voice cracked with regret.

The handcuffs clanged again, as he reached for her hands this time. The guard stepped forward and cleared his throat in a warning, and Hank pulled his hands back.

"Look at me, Avery," Hank said in a deep voice. "I didn't kill Wade."

"What?"

"I didn't kill him," Wade said again, his voice a hoarse whisper.

Avery gaped at him. Was this a last-minute attempt to save himself from death? "But…you told them you hated him, that you were glad you'd stabbed him."

He leaned closer over the table, his look feral. "I did stab him, but he was already dead when I stuck that blade in him."

"What?" Avery's head reeled. "Why didn't you tell the police that?"

"Because I thought *you* killed him," Hank hissed.

Avery gasped. "You…thought I killed him?"

"Yes." The word sounded as if it had been ripped straight from his gut. "He was in your room, and there was no one else there in the house. And you had a knife. It was bloody."

"What?" Avery looked down at her hands. "But I don't remember that."

Hank rubbed hand down his face. "I…I took it from you. You were…hysterical, in shock."

Avery tried to piece together the holes in her past. "But…I didn't kill him, Hank. At least I don't think I did."

Hank's eyes narrowed. "You said you blacked out?"

She had lost time, lost her memory. Because she'd stabbed Wade herself?

Her pulse thundered. Had she let Hank go to jail to cover for her?

God… "Hank, tell me the truth. Did you see me stab him?"

"No, not exactly." Hank rolled his hands into fists on the table, his scarred knuckles red from clenching his hands so tight. "But I heard him going into your room that night. I knew what he was going to do. I'd known it when Joleen left that morning and I'd been dreading it all day."

So had she.

"So I sneaked a knife under my pillow. But he tied me up like always. I lay there and heard the door open, and I got angry." His cheeks blushed with shame. "Then I heard you crying again, and I got madder and madder. He was a monster, and I was your big brother. I had to do something."

"But you did," Avery said, her heart aching as memories surfaced. "You tried to pull him off me before, and he beat you for it." She paused, struggling with the images hitting her. Wade on top of her. Wade holding her down.

Or was that another night? So many of them bled together.…

Nights of Wade shoving Hank against the wall and beating him with his belt. His fists. A wooden mallet. Anything he could get his hands on.

"I *wanted* to kill him," Hank said, his voice gaining force. "So I twisted in the bed until I got hold of that knife and cut myself free. But when I made it to your room, Wade was already bleeding on the floor. His eyes were bulging, and he wasn't breathing."

Avery's head swam. "He was already dead?"

Hank nodded. "I thought you'd stabbed him. You were crouched on the bed, crying and shaking. I tried to get you to stop crying, but you wouldn't. And you wouldn't talk, either. You just kept staring at the blood, and I heard the siren and was afraid they'd take you away, and you didn't deserve that."

A cold chill enveloped Avery. "Oh, Hank, what have we done?"

Silence fell between them, fraught with emotion. They were both lost in the horror of that night.

Finally Avery swiped at her tears. "This is unreal.... You went to jail for nothing. I should have come forward and told everyone what he'd done to me." Rage and pain suffused her for all Hank had lost. For what they'd both lost. "I'm so sorry.... We have to make this right. We have to get you out of here."

Despair settled on Hank's face, the scar on his temple stark beneath the harsh lighting. "It's too late now. My execution is already set."

She couldn't let him die for a crime he hadn't committed. "No, I'll find a way," she said. "I'll talk to your lawyer."

Hank grunted. "Not the one I had in the beginning. He didn't give a crap. But there is a new lady, just out of law school. She came to see me a few weeks ago."

"Did you tell her what you told me?"

Hank shook his head. "I was afraid they'd come after you and arrest you. There's no way I'd let you end up in this place."

Avery's throat burned with regret, yet her anger gave her strength. "What was this lawyer's name? I'll talk to the warden, and then I'll call her."

"It won't do any good," Hank said, defeat in his voice. "I told you, it's too late."

"No, it's not." Avery took a deep breath. "What was that lawyer's name?"

"Lisa Ellis," Hank mumbled. "But I'm telling you, it won't make any difference." He gestured around the room, then at the guard. "I know how things work in here."

Avery's voice gained conviction. "I'm not going to let you die for something you didn't do, Hank. I'll talk to that lawyer and if she can't help, I'll find someone who will."

Avery stood, anxious to make the phone call. Hank had given up hope long ago because she hadn't been there for him.

No one had.

It was time that changed.

JAXON IDENTIFIED HIMSELF to the warden, a chuffy bald man with thick dark brows and ropes of tattoos on his arms, and explained that he wanted to visit Hank Tierney.

"Yes, you can see him, but this is odd," Warden Unger said. "Tierney has only had one visitor in the past twenty years until today. Today he's had two."

Jaxon straightened his shoulders. "Who else came to see him?"

"His sister." The warden scratched his head. "Obviously with the execution date approaching, she wanted to say goodbye."

Or perhaps that lawyer Director Landers had mentioned had spoken with her.

The warden twirled the pen on his desk. "What brings you here?"

"My director wanted me to make sure the execution is still on."

Warden Unger nodded. "Good. Thought you might be working for that pansy-ass attorney out to get a stay."

"I take it that means you think Tierney is guilty."

Unger shrugged and dropped the pen. "A jury convicted him. My job is to make sure these animals in here don't slit each other's throats, not argue with the court."

A buzzer sounded on the warden's desk, and his receptionist's voice echoed over the speaker.

"Warden, Avery Tierney insists on seeing you right away."

Unger glanced at Jaxon and Jaxon nodded in agreement. "Send her in."

Jaxon had studied the files on the case before he'd driven to the prison. Avery Tierney had been the only person at the house when her brother murdered their foster father.

She was nine at the time, and according to the doctor who'd examined and interviewed her afterward, she'd been in shock and too traumatized to talk.

The door opened, and the warden's secretary escorted Avery Tierney in.

Nothing Jaxon had read in the file prepared him for the beautiful woman who stepped inside. Avery Tierney had been a skinny, homely-looking kid wearing hand-me-downs with scraggly, dirty brown hair and freckles. She'd looked lost, alone and frightened.

This Avery was petite with chocolate-brown eyes that would melt a man's heart and curves that twisted his gut into a knot.

Although fear still lingered in those eyes. The kind of fear that made a man want to drag her in his arms and promise her everything would be all right.

She looked back and forth between him and the warden. "Warden Unger," Avery said, her voice urgent. "You have to help me stop the execution and get my brother released from prison."

The warden cleared his throat. "Why would I do that, Miss Tierney?"

A pained sound ripped from Avery Tierney's throat. "Because he's innocent. He didn't kill Wade Mulligan."

Chapter Two

Jaxon forced himself not to react. Avery was obviously emotional over losing her brother, and desperate now that his execution was less than a week away.

Warden Unger gestured toward Jaxon. "This is Sergeant Jaxon Ward with the Texas Rangers. Sit down, Miss Tierney, and tell us what's going on."

Avery's brows pinched together as she glanced at Jaxon. "You came to help Hank?"

Jaxon gritted his teeth. "I came to talk to him," he said, omitting the fact that he'd actually come to confirm the man's guilt, not help him.

Avery didn't sit, though. She began to pace, rubbing her finger around and around her wrist as if it were aching.

His gaze zeroed in on the puckered scar there, and his gut tightened. It was jagged, ridged—maybe from a knife wound?

Was it self-inflicted or had someone hurt her?

AVERY TRIED TO ignore the flutter in her belly that Jaxon Ward ignited. She had never been comfortable with men, never good at flirting or relationships. And this man was so masculine and potent that he instantly made her nervous.

His broad shoulders and big hands looked strong and comforting, as if they could be a woman's salvation.

But big hands and muscles could turn on a woman at any minute.

Besides, she had to focus on getting Hank released. Sorrow wrenched her at the thought that he'd been imprisoned his entire life for a crime he hadn't committed.

"Miss Tierney?" Sergeant Ward said. "I understand you're probably upset about the execution—"

"Of course I am, but it's not that simple. I just talked to Hank and I know he's innocent."

That was the second time she'd made that statement.

"Miss Tierney," the warden said in a questioning tone, "I don't understand where this is coming from. You haven't visited your brother in all the time he's been incarcerated. And now after one visit, you want us to just believe he should be freed."

"I should have come to see him before," Avery said, guilt making her choke on the words. "I...don't know why I didn't. I was scared, traumatized when I was younger. I...blocked out what happened that night and tried to forget about it."

"You testified against your brother," Jaxon said. "You remembered enough to tell the police that you saw him stabbing Wade Mulligan."

A shudder coursed up her spine as she sank into the chair beside the Texas Ranger. "I know," she said, mentally reliving the horror. The blood had been everywhere. Hank had been holding the knife, his T-shirt soaked in Wade's blood.

"But Hank just told me what really happened." She gulped back a sob. "He said he found our foster father on the floor, already dead. He thought I killed him, so he covered for me."

Jaxon and the warden exchanged skeptical looks. "Hank is desperate, Miss Tierney," Jaxon said. "At this point, self-preservation instincts are kicking in. He'll say anything to convince the system to reevaluate his case. Anything to stay alive."

"But you don't understand—" Avery said.

"He confessed," Warden Unger said, cutting her off. "Besides, the psych reports indicated that your brother was troubled. Other foster parents testified that he was violent. Mulligan's own wife stated that Hank was full of rage."

"Yes, he hated Wade and so did I." Avery's anger mounted. "We both had good reason. Wade used to beat Hank, and he…" She closed her eyes, forcing the truth out. Words she'd never said before. "He abused me. Hank was only trying to protect me that night. He took beatings for me all the time."

Jaxon leaned forward. "Protecting you and hating his abuser give him motive for murder," he pointed out. "Although I'm surprised Hank's attorney didn't use that argument in his defense."

"So you read his file?" Avery asked.

Jaxon shrugged. "Briefly."

"It doesn't matter," Warden Unger said. "Hank Tierney confessed."

"Because he thought I killed Wade," Avery admitted in a broken voice. "That's the reason he confessed. He thought I stabbed Wade, and he didn't want me to go to jail."

JAXON'S PULSE JUMPED at the vehemence in her voice. "Why would he think that you killed Mulligan?"

Avery stared down at her fingers, then traced that scar on her wrist again, a fine sheen of perspiration breaking out on her forehead.

"Because Wade…was coming into my room that night." Avery's voice trembled. "Joleen, our foster mother, left earlier that day, and Hank and I both knew what that meant."

Jaxon had a bad feeling he knew as well, but he needed her to say it. "What did it mean?"

She visibly shuddered. "It meant we'd have a bad night," she said in a faraway voice. "That Wade would be drinking."

The pain in her eyes sent a shiver of rage through Jaxon. "He'd hurt you before?"

She nodded again. Which meant Hank could have planned the attack, that it was premeditated. According to the transcript of the case, Hank had never expressed any remorse for what he'd done.

Hell, Jaxon couldn't blame Hank. Knowing his foster father was hurting his sister could make a fourteen-year-old boy stab a man to death and not regret it.

Avery sucked in a shaky breath. "I tried locking the door, but that only made Wade madder and he tore through it with a hatchet. And that night…I heard him yelling at Hank. Hank tried to fight him, but he tied Hank in his room."

Jaxon's jaw ached from clenching it.

"Then I…heard the door open and…"

The images bombarding Jaxon made him knot his hands into fists. But he didn't want to frighten Avery, so he stripped the rage from his voice. "What happened then?" he asked softly.

She lifted her gaze, her eyes tormented. "I don't remember. I… Sometimes when Wade came in, I blacked out, just closed my eyes and shut out everything."

The warden was watching her with a skeptical look. But Jaxon had grown up in the system himself. He knew firsthand the horrors foster kids faced. The feelings of abandonment, of not being wanted. The abuse.

"What *do* you remember?" he asked.

She ran a hand through the long strands of her wavy hair. Hair the color of burnished copper. Hair that he suddenly wanted to stroke so he could soothe her pain.

"The next thing I remember was seeing Hank holding that knife." She straightened and brushed at the tears she didn't seem to realize she was crying. "But it could have happened the way he said. Someone else could have killed Wade. Then Hank came in and thought I did, so he stabbed him and took the blame to protect me."

"But you were the only two people in the house," Jaxon said. "You and Hank both said that."

Avery looked up at him with a helplessness that gnawed at his very soul. "But there had to be someone else," she said. "Hank only confessed because he thought I stabbed Wade. I can't let him go to the death chamber for protecting me."

Jaxon wanted to believe her, but there hadn't been signs of anyone else at the house.

And without evidence or proof of her story, there was no way to save her brother.

AVERY SENSED THE warden was not on her side. He'd obviously heard hundreds of inmates declare their innocence.

Death row inmates in the last stages of their lives probably always made a last-minute plea of innocence.

But she believed her brother and had to help him.

Because the person who'd really killed Wade Mulligan had escaped.

Her heart hammered.

What if I did kill him?

The thought struck Avery like a physical blow. Hank must have had a reason to think she did....

He'd mentioned that she had a knife.... She didn't remember that.

Did she have blood on her hands?

For a second panic seized her.

What if she discovered she had stabbed Wade, and that she'd let her brother take the fall?

Bile rose to her throat.

"Avery, are you all right?"

Sergeant Ward's gruff voice made her jerk her head up. His deep brown eyes were studying her with an intensity that sent tingles along her nerve endings. It was almost as if he were trying to see inside her head, trying to read her soul.

She felt naked. Vulnerable. Raw and exposed in a way she hadn't felt in years.

Because she'd just confessed about the abuse, which meant others would be asking questions. And if Hank's case were reopened, she would have to go public with her statement.

Shame mingled with nausea. Could she open herself up to that kind of publicity? Then everyone would know....

"I'd like to talk to Hank myself." Sergeant Ward turned to the warden. "Can I do that now?"

The warden's scowl cut Avery to the bone. "Sure. But you're wasting your time. In all the years Tierney has been here, this is the first time he's ever claimed innocence."

"What kind of prisoner has he been?" the Texas Ranger asked.

The warden pulled up his record on his computer. "A loner. Kept to himself. Got into fights a lot when he first got here." He scanned the notes. "Prison psychologist said he kept saying he was glad Mulligan was dead."

Avery's chest ached with the effort to breathe. "Was he abused in prison?"

The warden folded his hands on his desk. "Lady, this is a maximum-security facility. We do our best to protect the inmates, but we've got rapists, murderers, pedophiles and sociopaths inside these walls. They're caged up like animals and have a lot of testosterone and pent-up rage."

Avery bit her lip. She'd heard horror stories of what happened to prisoners, especially young men. And Hank had only been a teenager when he was arrested. Not able to defend himself.

"When he was sentenced, he was only fourteen." Sergeant Ward said. "Why didn't he receive psychiatric care and chance of parole?"

Warden Unger grunted and looked back at the computer. "The prosecuting attorney showed pictures of the gruesome, bloody crime scene, a dozen stab wounds altogether. That was enough for the jury to see that Tierney was violent and dangerous enough to be locked away forever."

Avery rubbed her wrist, a reminder of her past.

And how far she'd come.

At least she thought she'd survived. But she'd been living a lie. Never moving forward.

Ignoring her brother who'd fought and lied and risked his life to save her.

The system had failed them by placing them with the Mulligans.

Shouldn't the fact that she and Hank were being abused have factored in to the court's decision? Hadn't anyone argued for Hank that he'd been protecting himself and her?

JAXON STOOD, BODY TAUT. Avery Tierney was obviously upset and struggling over her visit with her brother. Had Hank Tierney manufactured this story as a last-ditch effort to escape a lethal injection?

Was he guilty?

An uneasy feeling prickled at Jaxon's skin. If Avery didn't remember the details of the murder, could she have stabbed her foster father, then blocked out the stabbing?

Damn. She'd only been a child. But if the man had been abusing her, and she'd fought, adrenaline could have surged enough for to fight the man and inflict a deadly stab wound.

Not likely. But not impossible.

The more believable scenario was the one the assistant district attorney had gone with when they'd prosecuted Tierney. They had concrete evidence, blood all over the boy and his hands, and those damning crime photos. For God's sake, Hank was holding the murder weapon and had admitted to stabbing Mulligan.

And Hank and Avery were the only two people in the house at the time.

"Talk to Hank and you'll see that he's telling the truth," Avery said. "Please, Sergeant, help me save him."

Man, that sweet voice of hers made him want to say yes. And those soulful, pain-filled eyes made him want to wipe away all her sorrow.

But he might not be able to do that. Not if Hank were guilty.

Avery touched his hand, though, and a warmth spread through him, a tingling awareness that sent a streak of electricity through his body.

And an awareness that should have raised red flags. She was a desperate woman. A woman in need.

A woman with a troubled past who might be lying just to save her brother.

He'd fallen into that trap before and almost gotten killed because of it. He'd vowed never to make that mistake again.

But the facts about the case bugged him. Considering the circumstances, the kid should have been given some leniency. Offered parole. He'd been fourteen. A kid trying to protect his sister.

Unless those circumstances hadn't been presented to the jury.

But why hadn't they?

His boss would know. But hell, Landers wanted Hank Tierney to be executed.

Because he believed Hank was a cold-blooded killer?

Or because he'd made a mistake and didn't want it exposed?

Chapter Three

Jaxon tried to reserve judgment on Hank Tierney as a guard escorted the inmate into the visitors' room, shackled and chained. Hank's shaved head, the scars on his arms and the angry glint in his eyes reeked of life on the inside.

A question flashed in Tierney's eyes when he spotted Jaxon seated at the table.

"Hello, Mr. Tierney, my name is Sergeant Jaxon Ward."

The man's thick eyebrows climbed. "What do you want?"

"To talk to you, Hank. I can call you Hank, can't I?"

The man hesitated, then seemed to think better of it and nodded. For a brief second, Jaxon glimpsed the vulnerability behind the tough exterior. But resignation, acceptance and defeat seemed to weigh down his body.

"I just talked to your sister, Avery." Jaxon watched for the man's reaction and noted surprise, then a small flicker of hope that made Tierney look younger than his thirty-four years. Maybe like the boy he'd been before he was beaten by Mulligan and he was locked away for life.

"I can't believe she called you. I just saw her." Emotions thickened his voice, a sign that he hadn't expected anything to come of their conversation.

That he hadn't expected anything out of life for a long time.

"She didn't," Jaxon said, knowing he couldn't offer Hank

Tierney false hope. In fact, all he really knew was that a jury had convicted him.

And that he and his sister might have concocted this story to convince a judge to order a stay of execution.

"I came at the request of my director. But your sister showed up at the warden's office while we were talking."

Cold acceptance resonated from Hank at that revelation. "So you came to make sure they stick the needle in me?"

He *was* world-weary.

Jaxon folded his arms and sat back, his professional mask in place. "I came for the truth. Your sister insists you're innocent."

Hank's chains rattled as he leaned forward. He ran his hand over his shaved head, more scars on his fingers evident beneath the harsh lights. When he finally looked back up at Jaxon, emotions glittered in the inmate's cold eyes. "You believe her?"

Jaxon scrutinized every nuance of Hank's expression and mannerisms. According to his files, he'd been an angry kid. And according to Avery, he'd been abused.

Twenty years in a cell had only hardened him more. The scars on his body and the harsh reality of prison conditions attested to the fact that he'd suffered more abuse inside. But judging from the size of his arms and hands, he'd learned to fight back.

"I don't know," Jaxon said. "I read the file. You confessed. You were convicted."

Hank shot up, rage oozing from his pores. "Then why did you come here?"

Because your sister has the neediest eyes I've ever seen.

He bit back the words, though. Avery Tierney had survived without him, and if she were the victim she professed to be, she might be lying now.

Worse, his boss wanted him to make sure the conviction wasn't overturned. Wouldn't look good on Director Landers if one of the cases that had made his career blew up and it was exposed that he'd sent an innocent man to prison on death row.

But something about the case aroused Jaxon's interest.

Because Avery had created doubt in his mind. Just a seed, but enough to drive him to want to know the truth.

"I had my reasons for confessing." Hank turned to leave, his chains rattling in the tense silence, his labored breath echoing in the room.

"Did you kill Wade Mulligan?" Jaxon asked bluntly.

Hank froze, his body going ramrod straight. Slowly he turned back to face Jaxon. The agony in his eyes made Jaxon's gut knot.

"I wanted him dead," Hank said, his voice laced with the kind of deep animosity that had been built from years of thinking about the monstrous things Mulligan had done. "I hated the son of a bitch." He shuffled back to the table and sank into the chair.

"Every night I lay there in that damned bed across the hall from Avery, staring at the ceiling just waiting. The old lady would take her pills and pass out. He'd wait a half hour or so, wait till the house was dark and he thought everyone was asleep." Hank traced one blunt finger over a fresh bruise on his knuckle. "But I couldn't sleep, and I knew Avery couldn't, 'cause we both knew what was coming."

Jaxon gritted his teeth.

"Then I'd hear that squeak of the door...." Hank's voice cracked. "At first, I was so scared I crawled in the closet and hid like a coward. But one night...I heard Avery crying and something snapped inside me." He balled his hands into fists, knuckles reddening with the force. "I couldn't stand it anymore. I had to do something."

Jaxon's stomach churned as he imagined Avery at nine, lying helpless at the mercy of that bastard. "What happened then?"

"I ran in and tried to drag him off her." Hank's voice shook, his eyes blurry with tears. "He knocked me off him and beat the hell out of me. Used a belt that night."

"It happened more than once?"

Hank dropped his head as if the shame was too much. "Yeah. After I started fighting back, I couldn't stop. But the beatings got worse. Then he started locking me up at night, tied me to the bed so I couldn't come in and stop him." He groaned. "I had to lie there like a trussed pig and listen to that grunting, the wall banging. I wanted to kill him so bad I imagined it over and over in my head."

Hank lapsed into silence, wrestling with his emotions. Sweat trickled down the side of his face.

"Tell me about the night of the murder," Jaxon finally said.

"The old lady was gone, left for a couple of days." Hank sucked in a deep breath, his eyes glazed as if he were thrust back in that moment. "I knew it was going to be bad that night, that he'd stay at it till dawn. So earlier, I hid a kitchen knife in my bed, under my pillow."

"He tied you up?"

Hank nodded. "But then Avery screamed, and I got mad. I twisted until I got that knife and cut the ropes." He jerked his hands as he might have done that night. "Then I tiptoed to the door and peeked into the hallway. Avery's door was cracked.... I could hear her crying...."

Jaxon swallowed. If he'd been Hank, he would have killed the animal, too.

"Then what happened?"

Hank pinched the bridge of her nose. "I had the knife in my hand, and I tiptoed across the hall. I wanted to sneak up on him, stop him once and for all. Make him feel pain for a change."

He paused, his expression twisting with horror. "But Mulligan was on the floor at the foot of Avery's bed. He...was staring up at the ceiling, his eyes wide like he was dead. Blood soaked his shirt, and he wasn't moving…."

Jaxon leaned forward, trying to visualize the scene. "He'd already been stabbed?"

Hank nodded. "Blood was on his shirt and the floor. One of his hands was covered in it where he'd grabbed his chest."

"Where was your knife?"

"In my hand." Hank slowly lifted his head, eyes cloudy with confusion. "Then I…saw Avery holding one."

Jaxon would have to check the police reports to see if there was any mention of a second knife. And he needed to look at the autopsy reports. "Then what happened?"

"She was pitiful, crying and rocking herself back and forth." He gulped. "So I ran over and took the knife from her. Then I wiped it off."

"If he was dead, why did you stab him?"

Hank gripped his thighs with his hands. "I don't know. Avery was sobbing, and I thought she'd get in trouble, and I couldn't let that happen. She was already suffering enough."

Jaxon felt for the kid and his situation.

"I wanted to cover for her. And I don't want to get her in trouble now."

"Let me worry about that," Jaxon said. "I just want the truth. Tell me about stabbing Mulligan."

Hank shrugged. "I was so mad. I had to make sure that monster never got up and hurt her again, so I lost it. All that rage and hate I had for him came out, and I went after him. I just started stabbing him, over and over and over."

Hank closed his eyes, pressed the heels of his hands against them and sat there for a long minute, his shoulders shaking.

Jaxon understood the man's—the boy's—rage. He'd felt helpless. Had felt responsible for his sister.

But there were still unanswered questions, pieces that

didn't fit. "Hank, what happened to the knife you brought into the room?"

He looked confused for a moment. "I...don't know. I think I dropped it when I ran to Avery."

"Did Avery have blood on her hands? On her night clothes?"

Hank shook his head. "I don't think so."

Jaxon breathed a small sigh of relief. If Avery had stabbed Mulligan, she would have had blood on her. She was only nine, too young and traumatized to have stabbed someone and clean up the mess.

Hank made another guttural sound in his throat. "Then Avery didn't kill him?"

"I doubt it," Jaxon said.

"That's the only reason I confessed, to keep her from being taken away." Hank gripped the edge of the table. "But if she didn't kill him, then I've spent my life in a cell for nothing."

Jaxon knew his boss wasn't going to like it. But he actually believed Hank Tierney.

"There's one major problem with your story," Jaxon pointed out. "You and Avery both claimed there was no one else in the house that night."

Hank pinched the bridge of his nose again. "There had to have been. Maybe someone came over after Mulligan tied me up in my room."

Jaxon gritted his teeth. That was a long shot. But it was possible.

Even if the man had killed Mulligan, Mulligan had deserved to die. Hell, Hank Tierney was a hero in Jaxon's book.

He didn't deserve a lethal injection for getting rid of a monster.

He should have been given a medal.

And if he hadn't killed Mulligan, then someone else had. Someone who was willing to let Hank die to protect himself.

AVERY WAITED IN an empty office for the Texas Ranger while he questioned Hank. She was still reeling in shock over her conversation with her brother.

She hadn't realized how much she'd missed him over the years. She'd been too busy trying to survive herself, working to overcome the trauma and shame of her abuse and the humiliation that had come from being a Tierney, born from a family of murderers.

Therapy had helped put her broken spirit and soul back together, although she still bore the physical and emotional scars.

But she had been free all this time.

Her brother had been labeled a murderer and spent most of his life behind bars, living with cold-blooded killers, rapists and psychopaths.

Hank didn't belong with them.

She had to talk to that lawyer. The guards had confiscated her cell phone when she arrived and would return it when she left, so she stepped to the door and asked the mental health worker if she could use the phone.

"I need to call my brother's lawyer."

The woman instructed her how to call out from the prison, and Avery took the card Hank had given her and punched the number. A receptionist answered, "Ellis and Associates."

"This is Avery Tierney, Hank Tierney's sister. I'd like to speak to Ms. Ellis."

"Hold please."

Avery tapped her shoe on the floor as she waited. Through the window in the office, she could see the open yard outside where the inmates gathered. Only a handful of prisoners were outside, four of them appearing to be engaged in some kind of altercation.

One threw a punch; another produced a shank made from something sharp and jabbed the other one in the neck. All hell broke loose as the others jumped in to fight, and guards raced out to pull them apart.

She shuddered, thinking about Hank being a target. How had he survived in here? He must have felt so alone, especially when his own sister hadn't bothered to come and visit him.

How could he not hate her?

"This is Lisa Ellis."

The woman's soft voice dragged Avery back to the present. She sounded young, enthusiastic. "This is Avery Tierney, Hank Tierney's sister. Hank told me that you came to see him and are interested in his case."

"Yes," Ms. Ellis said. "I've looked into it, but unfortunately I haven't found any evidence to overturn the conviction. And your brother wasn't very cooperative. In fact, he told me to let it go."

Avery traced a finger along the edge of the windowsill as she watched the guard hauling the injured inmate toward a side door. Blood gushed from his throat, reminding her of the blood on Hank's hands and Wade Mulligan's body.

"Miss Tierney?"

"Yes." She banished the images. "I just talked to Hank. We have to help him. He's innocent."

A heartbeat of silence. "Do you have proof?"

Avery's heart pounded. "No, but I spoke with a Texas Ranger named Jaxon Ward and he's going to look into it." At least she prayed he would.

"I read the files. You were the prime witness against your brother."

"I know, but that was a mistake," Avery said. "A horrible mistake. I was traumatized at the time and blocked out the details of that night."

"Now you've suddenly remembered something after all these years?" Her tone sounded skeptical. "Considering the timing, it seems a little too coincidental."

Frustration gnawed at Avery. The lawyer was right. Everyone would think she was lying to save her brother.

"I didn't exactly remember anything new," Avery said, although she desperately wished she did. "But I just spoke with Hank, and we had a long talk about that night. It turns out that he confessed to the murder because he thought I killed Wade."

Another tense silence. "Did you?"

Avery's breath caught. That was a fair question. Others would no doubt ask it.

And if she had killed Wade… Well, it was time she faced up to it.

"I don't know," she said honestly. "I don't think so. But Hank said when he came into my bedroom, Wade was already lying on the floor with a knife wound in his chest. He saw me crouched on the bed, crying, and he thought I killed Wade in self-defense, so when the police came, he confessed to cover for me."

"That's some story," Ms. Ellis said. "Unfortunately without proof, it'll be impossible to convince a judge to stop the execution and reopen the case."

Despair threatened to overwhelm Avery. She understood the lawyer's point, but she had to do something.

"Can't you argue that someone else came in, killed Wade Mulligan and left?"

"With you in the room?"

Avery closed her eyes, panic flaring. If only she could remember everything that had happened that night…

"The social worker and doctor who examined me afterward can testify that I was traumatized, but that it was possible."

"I'm sorry, Miss Tierney, I want to help. But I need more."

Determination rallied inside her. Then she'd get more.

Footsteps pounded the floor, and she looked up and saw

the handsome-as-sin Texas Ranger appear in the doorway. His square jaw was solid, strong, set. Grim.

His eyes were dark with emotions she couldn't define.

He didn't believe Hank. He wasn't going to help her.

She could see it in his eyes.

Hank's scarred face haunted her. She'd let him down years ago when she told the police she'd seen him stab Wade. And then again when she stayed away from the prison. When she let holidays and birthdays pass without sending cards or writing or paying him a visit.

If Ranger Ward wouldn't investigate, she'd do some digging around on her own.

Chapter Four

Jaxon's insides were knotted with tension. He believed Hank Tierney.

But he would be in hot water with his boss if he challenged his opinion and the verdict that had landed Tierney on death row.

Landers also knew Jaxon's past and would question his objectivity regarding the situation. Hell, the man had practically dragged Jaxon from the gutter himself.

Jaxon owed him.

But…Avery had sounded upset, and the way she described that night sounded so heart wrenching that she couldn't have made up what had happened or been acting.

Could she?

Unless…she'd been so traumatized that the details of the evening were distorted to the point that she believed the story she'd told.

Or…there always the possibility that she and her brother had concocted this story at the last minute to create enough reasonable doubt that the governor would have to grant a stay and retry the case. And if they both stuck to their story, it was possible they could garner enough sympathy to convince a jury that Hank was innocent. That they were both victims.

Which he believed they were.

Avery dropped the phone into its cradle. "You aren't going to help me, are you?"

Jaxon's lungs tightened. Damn if she didn't have the sweetest voice.

He scrubbed his hand over the back of his neck. What the hell was wrong with him? When had he become such a sap?

"I will investigate," Jaxon said, knowing he was jeopardizing his career, but that he had to know the truth. "I'd like to talk to the foster mother you lived with at the time."

Avery's eyes widened in surprise. "I have no idea where she is. At the trial, she said Hank and I ruined her life."

They had ruined her life? "What happened to you after the trial?"

"They placed me in a group home. I never heard from her again."

"She and her husband should have been prosecuted for child abuse and endangerment." And the old man for rape.

"Did you tell the social worker about the abuse?" he asked.

Avery averted her face. "No. I was too ashamed at the time. I thought...that I did something wrong. And Wade said if I told, he'd kill me and Hank."

He wished Wade were alive so he could kill him himself.

Worse, if the social worker hadn't documented evidence of abuse, then it was Avery and Hank's word against a dead man's. A prosecutor would argue that they'd invented the story to save Hank.

But he didn't think Avery was lying about the abuse. That kind of pain was hard to fake.

Besides, any woman who stood by and allowed abuse of any kind to take place in her home was just as guilty as the perpetrator.

Although psychologists argued women were too afraid physically of their abusers to leave or stand up to them. And they often felt trapped by financial circumstances.

Worse, if a woman sent her abuser to jail, when he was released he often went straight home and took his anger out on her all over again.

It was a flawed system, but if it were his child, he'd die to protect him or her.

"I'll find her," Jaxon said. "I'd also like to speak with the social worker who placed you and Hank in that home."

Because that social worker should have realized what was happening and stopped it.

AVERY COULDN'T BELIEVE the Ranger's words or that his voice sounded sincere. But something about the man's gruff exterior and those deep-set dark, fathomless eyes, told her that he was a man of his word.

Not like any other man she'd ever known.

Don't believe him, a little voice in her head whispered. *Men who make promises either lie or have their own agenda.*

He'll want something in return.

She was not the kind of girl to do favors like that.

"You really are going to talk to them?" she asked.

He tipped his Stetson, a sexy move that spoke of respect and manners and…made her heart flutter with female nerves.

Good heavens. She had to get a grip. Jaxon Ward was a Texas Ranger. And she needed his help for Hank.

Nothing more.

He took a step closer, his masculine scent wafting toward her and playing havoc with her senses. "Hank said he stabbed Wade Mulligan, but that he was already dead. If you didn't deliver the deadly blow and Hank didn't, that means there was someone else in the house." The silver star on his chest glittered in the harsh lights. "Who else might have wanted the man dead?"

Avery had desperately tried to forget everything about

the man. But if she wanted to help Hank, she had to confront the past.

"Avery, can you think of anyone?"

"His wife," she said, her heart thundering. "If she knew he was coming into my room, maybe she tried to stop him."

Jaxon's expression was grim. "That makes sense, but didn't she have an alibi for that night?"

Avery's head swam. "She claimed she was at her mother's." Panic began to claw at her chest. "Maybe Joleen lied about going to her mother's. Or she could have come back for some reason, and she saw Wade tie up Hank and come into my room. Then she slipped in and killed him."

Although even as she suggested the possibility, despair threatened. The problem with that theory was that Joleen hadn't cared for her or Hank.

She certainly hadn't loved them enough to kill her husband for them.

JAXON GRIMACED. DISCUSSING the case would definitely reopen old wounds for Avery, but questions had to be asked and answered. "Do you know if Mrs. Mulligan continued to take in foster children after her husband was murdered?"

"I have no idea what happened to her," Avery said.

"What about the social worker who placed you with the Mulligans? What was her name?"

Avery rubbed her forehead as if thinking back. "I...think it was Donna. No, Delia. I don't know her last name."

"There should be records," Jaxon said. "What do remember about her?"

Avery shrugged. "Not much. She gave me candy on the ride to the Mulligans' the day she dropped us off." Her voice cracked. "But I don't remember her coming back to visit."

Jaxon bit back a response. "Did she testify at your brother's trial?"

Avery rubbed the scar around her wrist. "I don't think

so. But I was so young that they didn't let me inside for some of the trial."

That made sense.

"I'll pull the transcripts from the trial and review them, then question her."

Avery squared her shoulders. "I'd like to go with you to see her."

He hesitated. "I'm not sure that's a good idea."

Avery folded her arms, a stubborn tilt to her chin. "I may have been a child then, Sergeant, but I'm not anymore. My testimony put my brother in prison, and got him the death penalty. Now that I know he's innocent, I have to make things right."

Jaxon lowered his voice. "Avery, do you think it's possible that Hank twisted the truth because he's afraid to die?"

She shook her head. "No. Hank's not like that. He always owned up to things he did wrong. Even if it meant he'd be punished for it. Besides, he just said that he confessed because he thought I killed Wade."

Oddly it sounded as though Hank Tierney had character, that he wasn't the bad seed the prosecutor had painted him to be.

And if a jury heard his testimony now and heard Avery's story, they might let Hank Tierney go.

So why hadn't the D.A. and Tierney's defense attorney pleaded not guilty and put the kid on the stand?

Dammit, he needed to see the autopsy report for Wade Mulligan. If someone else had delivered the fatal stab wound before Hank Tierney had unleashed his rage, it might show up in the autopsy report.

AVERY'S PALMS BEGAN to sweat at the idea of dredging up the details of the past. Already she felt drained from the day's visit with Hank and now this Texas Ranger.

And if she helped Hank—and she *had* to help him—this

was only the beginning. Everyone in the town—hell, everyone in the state—would know her sordid story.

Taking a deep breath to fortify her resolve, she lifted her chin. "Please. It's time for me to face the past. Maybe seeing Joleen Mulligan and the social worker will jog my memory of that night."

"That's possible." Sergeant Ward's dark eyes met hers. "But are you ready for that?"

No. She wanted to run as fast as she could and as far away as possible. But Hank's troubled voice claiming he was innocent, that he'd taken the rap to save her from arrest, echoed in her ears. There was no way she could allow him to be put to death when he'd confessed to protect her.

"Yes. I have to do this, Sergeant."

"All right. Give me your number, and I'll call you when I locate them."

Avery recited her cell number, and he entered it into his phone.

The dark, handsome Ranger tilted his head to the side. "One thing, Avery—I will look into Hank's story, but I can't promise anything. It's almost impossible to get a murder conviction overturned this late in the game."

"It's not a game," Avery said, her senses prickling. "This is my brother's life."

A heartbeat of silence stretched between them. "I know that. But I don't want you to get your hopes up." He pierced her with a dark look. "And if I find out either of you is lying and using me, I won't hesitate to tell the judge that, either."

Her heart hammered against her breastbone. "Hank and I aren't lying," she said. "Hank didn't kill Wade Mulligan. That means that the real killer has been walking around free for twenty years thinking he got away with it. And I can't live with that."

A muscle twitched in his strong jaw. "You may have to. Sometimes the justice system fails."

Yes, it had done so twenty years ago.

But she'd do everything within her power to change that now.

JAXON'S PHONE BUZZED as soon as he left the prison. His director.

Still contemplating what to tell him, Jaxon let the phone roll to voice mail.

Wind whistled across his skin as he climbed into his SUV and pulled from the parking spot. He'd worked in law enforcement for ten years, yet the razor wire and armed guards made sweat bead on his skin. He liked the law, thought the system worked for the most part.

But occasionally a case went wrong. An innocent victim fell through the cracks.

Hank Tierney had been locked up since he was a teenager. Should he have been free all this time?

Had his life been stolen from him by someone who'd murdered his foster father, then walked around free for twenty years while he lived in hell?

Chapter Five

On the way to Cherokee Crossing, Jaxon stopped for lunch at a barbecue joint, wolfed down a sandwich, then looked up the number for the attorney interested in Tierney's case. The receptionist patched him through immediately.

"Sergeant Ward, I talked to Avery Tierney earlier. She said you were investigating the murder conviction."

"I am," Jaxon admitted. "Did you find anything that might exonerate Hank?"

"Nothing specific," Ms. Ellis replied. "I just had a feeling when I read the story that there was more to it. Foster-care kids get bum deals. I wanted to know more."

"You may be right."

"Listen," Ms. Ellis said, "if there's anything I can do to help, let me know. If that man is innocent as his sister claims, he deserves justice."

He agreed with her on that. "Thank you. Call me if you learn anything that might be helpful."

He hung up, then used his tablet to access police databases and search for Joleen Mulligan. It didn't take long to find her. She had a rap sheet.

Two DUIs and an arrest for possession of narcotics. She'd also been dropped as a foster parent after Mulligan's death, so she'd resorted to government assistance and project housing.

Jaxon phoned a friend with social services—Casey Chambers, a young woman in her twenties whose parents had been killed when she was twelve, throwing her into the system. She'd seen enough of it to want to help other kids get out like she had.

"Hey, Jaxon, what can I do for you?"

"I need some background information on a case that came through the social service agency twenty years ago."

"What's this about?"

"The Hank Tierney murder conviction."

"You're looking in to that?" Casey made a soft sound in her throat. "I've seen the protestors, and I heard some young lawyer was asking questions, too. Is that true?"

"Yeah. I was at the prison and some questions have come up regarding the conviction. I need contact information for the social worker who placed Hank and his sister, Avery, in the Mulligans' home. Her first name was Delia."

"That was a long time ago and the agency has a pretty high turnover rate. Burnout and all."

"I understand. But can you find it?"

"I'll see what I can do and get back with you."

"Thanks, Casey."

"Jaxon, what do you think? I read about the murder and the guy's confession. He admitted to stabbing the man. But something doesn't ring right to me."

Avery's pain-filled eyes taunted him. "I know. That's why I want to talk to the social worker."

A hesitation. "Jax?"

"Don't repeat that to anyone," he said. "Just get me that information."

"You got it."

The waitress brought his check, and he paid the bill and left her a nice tip, then drove toward the courthouse. The land seemed even more deserted with winter taking its toll.

Everything looked desolate, deserted, dry, almost like a ghost town.

Cherokee Crossing looked like a throwback in a Western movie with a bar/saloon in the heart of town, and a tack-and-boot store beside it. Life moved slower here. Residents told stories about the Cherokee Indians being the dominant tribe in the area, and the canyon that had literally and figuratively divided the Native Americans and early settlers.

The town had been built to bridge that gap.

Jaxon parked in front of the county courthouse, noting the parking lot was nearly empty. It was four-thirty; people were heading home for the day. He parked next to a pickup, then strode up the sidewalk to the courthouse steps. He identified himself, then went through security and headed to the clerk's office.

He greeted the secretary, reminding himself to use his charm. Death penalty cases were always controversial and stirred emotional reactions on all sides.

Alienating people would not get him what he wanted. Avery's tormented expression haunted him. He hoped to hell he wasn't being a sucker and being lured into believing an act.

Maybe the social worker could shed some light on the situation. He also needed to review the trial transcripts, study the way the lawyers handled the case, make sure nothing was overlooked or evidence hadn't gotten lost, misplaced or intentionally omitted.

Roberta, the clerk in charge of records, was always friendly and knew more about the goings-on in the courthouse than anyone else. She'd also worked with the court system for thirty years.

Jaxon had only been a year older than Hank Tierney when Hank was arrested. That was probably one reason he remembered the case so well.

It had been all over the news. Jaxon's uncle, the only living relative he'd had at the time, was disabled and had watched the story with him, then had a come-to-Jesus talk with Jaxon. He'd told him he was going to end up like Hank Tierney one day if he didn't get his act together.

Unable to raise him, that uncle had shipped Jaxon to a military school, where he'd learned to be a man. He'd hated it at first.

But looking back, he now saw that that school had saved him from going down the wrong path.

"Hi, Roberta, I need some help. Can you get me a copy of the transcripts of Hank Tierney's trial twenty years ago?"

Roberta's eyebrows climbed. "The Tierney man who's about to die?"

"Yes. My director wants me to review the matter because of some young lawyer looking to get the conviction overturned."

Roberta sighed. "I always felt sorry for that boy and girl. Folks said the boy was scary, that he stabbed that man a bunch of times, but if you ask me, something else was going on in that house. Something nobody wanted to talk about."

"You remember the trial?" Jaxon asked.

"Of course." She reached for a set of keys in her drawer. "Never forget how terrified that poor child looked when the reporters pounced on her. That young'un was scared to death. Something bad happened to her, I tell you. Children don't look like that unless they've seen real-life monsters."

True.

She ambled around the side of the desk. "Those files are old, Sergeant. They'll be archived downstairs."

"That's fine. Can you find them and make a copy for me?"

"Sure. But it might take a few minutes."

"No problem. I'll be glad to wait."

She maneuvered her bulk toward the door and walked down the hall. Jaxon phoned Avery. She answered on the third ring. "Hello."

"Avery, this is Sergeant Jaxon Ward. I found an address for Joleen Mulligan. I'm going to visit her tonight."

Her breathing rattled in the silence that fell between them. "I'll call you after I talk to her," he said.

"No," Avery said in a shaky voice. "I want to go with you."

Jaxon gritted his teeth. "Are you sure you're up for that?"

"No," she said softly. "But I'm the reason my brother is in this mess. It's my place to get him out."

A wealth of guilt underscored her words.

Jaxon found himself wanting to erase that guilt. But that might not be possible. Chances were slim that they could get her brother's execution postponed, and even slimmer that they could prove him innocent and free him.

AVERY LOWERED HER head between her legs and inhaled slow, even breaths just as her therapist had instructed to do to ward off panic attacks.

That had been years ago, although occasionally old fears swept over her when she least expected it. The least little thing could trigger a reaction.

A sudden dimming of lights. A noise. The sound of someone breathing too hard. The smell of smoke or…body sweat.

And cologne, the one Mulligan wore. The musty smell hadn't mixed well with the rancid odor of his beer breath.

"Avery?"

The Texas Ranger's voice startled her, jerking her back to reality. "Yes."

"Do you want me to pick you up, or do you want me to meet you somewhere?"

Her first reaction was to meet him. She didn't like to be in enclosed spaces with men. But Jaxon Ward was a law officer, and he was trying to help her.

He'd think she was strange, rude, maybe paranoid or unstable if she balked at riding in the car with him.

"I'm almost to my house if you want to meet me there."

"Fine. I'm at the county courthouse. It'll probably be a while before I leave. I'll pick you up in an hour."

"That works." She needed that hour to pull herself together. Maybe do some yoga to relax and focus her energy on her well-being.

On the fact that she had survived the Mulligan abuse and family years ago, and she was an adult now. Joleen Mulligan couldn't hurt her.

She wouldn't let her.

BY THE TIME Roberta returned with the files, it was already getting dark outside.

"I had to dig deep," Roberta said. "But you have to sign in to have access, and that took a while. The guard in charge asked a half dozen questions. Said you were the second person in two weeks to ask for a copy of the trial transcripts and copy of the police investigation report."

"Did he mention who else made the request?"

"That lawyer, Ellis. Said she was gonna talk to Hank Tierney, too."

"Thanks, Roberta," Jaxon said. "You take care."

Roberta caught him by the arm before he could leave. "You do right by them, Mr. Jaxon, you hear me? They were just kids when all that went down."

She was obviously sympathetic to Avery and her brother.

"I will," he said, although he couldn't make any promises to her, either. When Landers found out what he was up to, he might pull him from the case.

Or fire his butt.

Tension knotted his shoulders as he carried the file through the building and outside to his SUV. The sky had turned a dismal gloomy gray while he was inside, the sound of thunder rumbling.

Texas temperatures could drop quickly, and the chill of the night was setting in.

He checked his phone for Avery's address as he climbed into his SUV, his pulse quickening when he realized she lived only a few miles from the government-funded project housing where Joleen Mulligan had spent the past few years.

As he expected, traffic was thin. The storm clouds gathered and rolled over the horizon, making it look bleak for the night. He maneuvered through the small town, around the square, then turned down Birch Drive, a street lined with birch trees.

The houses were small, rustic and quaint, but even with winter, the yards looked well-kept. A few had toys indicating small children, a Western theme evident in the iron mailboxes that all sported horses on the top of the barn-shaped boxes.

Avery's house was the last one on the right, with flower boxes and a windmill in the front yard. He couldn't see the back, but it was fenced in, which surprised him since the land didn't back up to anything else. Then again, she might have a dog.

He pulled up behind a Pathfinder and shifted into Park, then climbed out, reminding himself that he was here on a job.

Not because meeting Avery Tierney sparked an attraction that he hadn't felt in a long time.

Hell, the woman had been abused as a child. That fact alone warned him to keep his distance. He had no idea what kind of scars she carried inside her, but he'd bet his life trusting men wasn't high on her list.

A bad side effect of foster life—kids grew up learning not

to get attached. They were shuffled around so much, and it hurt too much to leave friends and people behind.

Besides, Avery was a case, nothing more. At least if he investigated, maybe he could sleep without those wounded, pain-filled eyes haunting him, telling him that he should have done something other than accept everyone's word that Hank Tierney deserved to die.

He punched the brass doorbell, then heard footsteps clattering inside. Seconds later, Avery opened the door.

He grew very still when he saw her pale face. Obviously today's visit at the prison had done a number on her.

What would facing the woman who should have protected her from that monster Mulligan do to her tonight?

AVERY PASTED ON a brave face, determined not to let Sergeant Ward see how the idea of confronting Joleen Mulligan was affecting her.

"Are you ready?"

She clutched her purse strap and nodded, but her heart was pounding as she locked the front door and followed him to his vehicle. She reached for the door handle and startled when he beat her to it and opened it for her.

Her nerves raw, she twisted her head up to look at him.

"I'm just opening the door for you," he said. "Relax, Avery. I'm trying to help you."

"Why?" The question flew from her mouth before she could stop herself from asking.

His dark eyes met hers, a sea of emotions swimming in the depths. She knew nothing about him except that he'd come to see Hank today.

She didn't even know the reason for his visit.

"Because I want justice served," he said in a gruff voice. "If it turns out your brother is innocent, I'll do whatever I can to free him. If it turns out he's guilty or if he's lying and using me, I'll watch while he dies."

His words hit her like a physical blow. Yet she admired his honesty.

If a man said what he meant, then maybe he'd do what he said.

She was counting on that.

Chapter Six

Jaxon wasn't sure if he made Avery nervous or if it was just the situation. He probably shouldn't have been so harsh. But he had to be honest.

Besides, he was fighting his own attraction toward her. Trying not to let her sweet but tortured look tear at his heart and make him do something he'd regret.

Like start to care for her.

Caring was way too dangerous for a man who lived his life working case to case. Besides, the only thing he knew about families was that they were messed up. Couples stood and made promises and vows that they didn't keep. Men strayed. Women strayed. Both got bored with each other.

The kids suffered in the end.

He didn't intend to travel down that path.

"Sergeant Ward?"

Then again, if he wanted her to be more comfortable, maybe they shouldn't be so formal. "Why don't you call me Jaxon, Avery?"

She gave him a wary look. "All right, Jaxon. Does Joleen know we're coming?"

"No. I didn't want to give her a chance to decline talking to me."

"She probably would, you know."

"Yeah, I do." He threaded his fingers through his hair as

he made the turn onto the road leading to Joleen's. Scrub brush, dry parched land and ranch land stretched out for miles, but the development had been built close to town for the residents' convenience.

He turned into the complex, scrutinizing the beat-up trucks and weathered cars scattered in the parking lot. A group of construction workers had gathered at one end by two trucks parked close together. Other families were grilling burgers while the children played tag.

"Joleen lives here?" Avery asked, surprise in her voice.

He nodded. "Apparently she lost her house after her husband's murder."

"I...didn't know."

Jaxon glanced at her with a frown. "Don't feel bad for her. Apparently she got some DUIs and had a drug arrest. Not to mention the fact that she didn't take care of you and your brother as she should have." And that was putting it mildly.

Avery nodded, her long hair spilling around her shoulders as she turned to look out the window.

"You want to tell me about her before we go in?"

She shrugged. "She was just one in a long line. But just like always, I hoped this one would be different." A bitter laugh escaped her. "But it was worse."

"Did she hurt you?"

Avery's sigh filled the silence. "She didn't hit us," she said softly. "She just...sat and drank and watched."

"Just as bad," Jaxon said.

Avery sucked in a sharp breath and reached for the door handle. "I'm not that scared little girl anymore," she said, her voice filled with determination. "In fact, this visit is long overdue."

AVERY WRESTLED WITH her nerves as they walked up the sidewalk. All the units were identical. The complex was situated next to the little store on the corner so residents could walk if they didn't own an automobile.

She was grateful Joleen wasn't still living in that run-down house where she and Hank had lived with the Mulligans. She hoped they'd burned down the place.

Jaxon knocked on the door while she studied the surroundings. Dirt marred the doorstep, and the flowers in the hanging basket had been dead for ages. Joleen had never been a housekeeper, one of the things that had triggered Wade's temper. He'd ranted that since he paid the bills, the least she could do was wash the dishes and have a meal on the table when he got home from work.

Considering the fact that her grocery money paid for her booze and her meals had mostly consisted of vodka, Joleen hadn't cared if any of them went hungry.

Jaxon knocked again, and finally they heard footsteps shuffling. The door screeched open, and Joleen peeked outside. Avery bit back a gasp at the woman's stark features.

The years and alcohol hadn't been kind to Joleen. Dark circles lined her glazed, bloodshot eyes; her skin looked yellow, deep wrinkles sagging around her chin, mouth and eyes.

Her graying eyebrows drew together in a frown. "What you want?"

"We need to talk to you," Jaxon said.

She pinched her lips together as she glared at Avery. "Who are you?"

"It's me, Avery Tierney," Avery said.

"Go away," Joleen snarled. "I don't have anything to say to you."

Jaxon caught the door when she tried to close it. "Actually it's Sergeant Ward with the Texas Rangers. And you do need to let us in."

Joleen ran a shaky hand through her scraggly hair, her eyes piercing Avery. "You got a lot of nerve showing up here after what you did to my family."

Jaxon shouldered his way past her, and Avery followed, stunning Joleen. She staggered back toward the couch in the den as if to escape them. The strong scent of booze assaulted Avery, mingling with the musty odor of the apartment, which looked as if it hadn't been cleaned in months. Dirty laundry, magazines and food-crusted dishes were everywhere. A coffee cup with something moldy in it sat on the coffee table beside a plate dried with eggs.

"We need to ask you some questions," Jaxon said.

Joleen picked up her tumbler and swirled the vodka around. "Why you coming around?" she asked Avery. "You want me to say I'm sorry your brother's about to get the needle for what he done?"

"My brother is innocent," Avery said.

"The hell you say," Joleen muttered. "You saw him stab my Wade."

"That's true," Avery said. "But I talked to Hank, and he told me that your husband was already dead when he stabbed him."

A bitter laugh escaped the woman. "Yeah, he would say that now that he's going to die—"

"Mrs. Mulligan," Jaxon interrupted sharply, "I need you to tell me what you remember about that day."

Joleen huffed, then tossed back a swallow of her drink. "Why? You trying to get that boy off?"

"I'm simply verifying the facts," Jaxon said. "So the sooner you answer my questions, the sooner we'll be out of your hair. Then you can get back to whatever you were doing."

Which would be finishing the bottle, Avery thought.

Joleen's hand shook as she reached for a lighter and pack of cigarettes on the table. "Got up same as usual. Wade went to work at the garage like always. I got a call from my mama saying she was ill and needed help." She tapped the pack against her hand, pulled out a cigarette and lit it. Once she exhaled the smoke, she continued, "I left Hank in charge." Another bitter laugh. "It was a mistake ever trusting that kid. Something was off about him."

"What? Because he was angry?" Avery said. "He had a right to be angry. We were tossed from house to house, and you and your husband made it clear that the only reason you took us in was to get that government check each month."

"We took you in 'cause nobody else wanted you," Joleen roared back. "And after what happened, I can see why. Hank was a mean kid, violent." Her hand shook as she took another drag on the cigarette. "I was so scared of him I used to lock my door every night."

Avery bit her tongue to keep from defending her brother. "You closed your door when you were passed out so Wade wouldn't come in and bother you. You closed it so you wouldn't have to hear what he was doing to me."

"You always were a little troublemaker," Joleen snarled. "Flaunting yourself in front of him. Asking for it."

"I was nine years old. I never asked for anything," Avery said. "Except for a home and a family. One that didn't use and abuse me."

"You ungrateful snit," Joleen quipped. "You wanted Wade to come in there, wanted him to love you. That's why he did it."

"He did it because you let him," Avery snapped. "You didn't want him touching you, so you let him turn to me for that."

Joleen's eyes blazed with rage. "I was afraid of him just like I was afraid of Hank."

Avery was trembling all over. She started to retaliate, but Jaxon caught her hand and squeezed it. His soothing look gave her comfort.

Still, all the anger and hurt and humiliation she'd felt over the years threatened to make her explode.

JAXON WANTED TO pull Avery into his arms and comfort her. He also wanted to get her as far away from this horrible excuse of a woman as he could. To protect her from the woman's vicious accusations.

But he'd come here for answers, and he didn't intend to leave without them.

"Why exactly were you afraid of Hank?" Jaxon asked.

"Because that kid was mean as a snake," Joleen growled.

"Hank wasn't mean," Avery said. "He was angry at you and your husband for the way you treated us."

"We gave you food and a roof over your head," Joleen snapped. "But you didn't appreciate anything."

Avery started to protest again, but Jaxon gave her a warning look. "Mrs. Mulligan, did your husband ever hit you?"

The woman tapped ashes into a dirty coffee cup. "No, but he came at me a couple of times."

Avery's eyes widened, but she bit back a response.

"Did your husband ever hit Hank?" Jaxon continued.

Joleen tossed back the rest of her vodka. "He had to," she muttered. "Kids need discipline, and that boy needed plenty of it."

"Where were you when these beatings occurred?"

"Making dinner or taking care of the house."

Avery's sigh suggested the woman was lying, that she'd probably been passed out.

"How about Avery?" Jaxon asked. "Did Wade ever hurt her?"

Joleen fidgeted, stubbed out her cigarette and poured herself another drink. "My husband was good to her," she said when she finally answered. "He loved Avery. That was his only flaw. Then those kids turned on him, and cost me everything. My Wade. My house. It's their fault I ended up here."

Anger surged through Jaxon. "Wade loved Avery so much that he molested her?"

Joleen jumped up, shoes clacking as she paced in front of the couch. "You got a lot of damn nerve speaking ill of the dead. That boy killed him, that's all there is to it." She swung her hand toward the door. "Now get the hell out."

Avery stood, rubbing her hands down her jeans as if she couldn't wait to leave. Jaxon stood as well, but he fisted his hands by his sides to keep from shaking the woman. She was a pathetic drunk, but that didn't excuse the fact that she'd allowed her husband to mistreat Hank and Avery.

"You said you went to see your mother. Is there anyone who can verify that you were with her all night?"

"You," Joleen shouted. "You trying to make me look bad? Like I killed Wade?"

"Just answer the question," Jaxon said.

Joleen crossed her arms. "My mama could. But she's dead."

"Was she in the hospital at the time?" Jaxon asked.

"No, at home."

"I suppose she lived alone?"

Joleen nodded. "Now, I'm done with you. If you wanted to pin this on me, you're way off. Hank killed Wade, and he's going to die for it."

Avery's expression bordered between rage and disgust. "I should have known you wouldn't help, just like you stood by and let your husband molest me. You're nothing but a sorry drunk, Joleen."

Joleen lunged toward Avery, but Jaxon stepped in front of Joleen to prevent her from touching Avery. "She's right," Jaxon said in a low voice. "In fact, if Hank did kill your husband, I don't blame him. The legal system got it wrong this time. They should have put you in jail as an accomplice to child abuse, child endangerment and rape." He balled his hands into fists. "And I'm going to do everything I can to see that the truth is exposed and that Hank Tierney goes free."

Barely able to control his rage, Jaxon coaxed Avery toward the door, before he strangled the woman to death himself.

Avery sank into the passenger seat, her heart hammering.

When she was little, she'd been scared of Joleen, not because she'd ever hit her, but she'd yelled and cursed and said horrible things to her. Had told her she was worthless and that was the reason no family wanted her.

And after Wade started coming into the room at night, she'd accused Avery of being a dirty girl.

She had *felt* dirty back then. Had felt as though she must have done something wrong to have brought that man to her bed.

Looking back, she realized that she hadn't done anything wrong. She was a child caught in a terrible situation.

In fact, she'd covered herself in clothes, long baggy shirts and sweatpants.

Anything to keep him from looking at her.

But it hadn't made a difference.

"Are you all right?" Jaxon asked as he slid into the seat beside her.

Avery leaned her head on her hand. "Yes. I...can't believe I used to be afraid of her. That I let her make me feel like I was nothing. She's pathetic."

"Yes, she is." Jaxon angled himself toward her. "I know it took a lot of courage for you to face her."

His praise nearly brought her to tears. She'd grown so accustomed to people being cruel to her or judging her by her past that when someone treated her with kindness, it touched her deeply.

Jaxon started the engine. "She was lying. She knew her husband was coming into your room."

"Of course she did, and she allowed it to happen," Avery

said. "Like I said, she didn't want him touching her, so she was happy to let him use me."

A muscle ticked in his jaw. "She might have not minded," he admitted. "Then again, if she was afraid of him, maybe she sneaked back and killed him, then let Hank take the fall."

"You think that's possible?"

"I think she might be more cunning than you gave her credit for." And if she had killed Mulligan, she needed to pay.

Chapter Seven

As Jaxon drove away from the complex, he contemplated the theory that Joleen had actually lied about being with her mother or returned home that night. Money hadn't been a motive.

But she could have come in, realized her husband was at it again and snapped.

Or could she have planned it—lied and said she was going to take care of her mother, waited till night, then sneaked back and stabbed him.

Maybe Avery had witnessed the murder and been so traumatized that she'd blocked it out. When Hank had seen Wade dead on the floor, he'd assumed his sister had stabbed Mulligan, and lied to protect her.

The scenario made sense. Not that he could sell it to a judge without proof.

More questions nagged at him. If Joleen had been drinking as much back then as she was now, would she have been able to pull off a murder without Avery or Hank knowing she was in the house?

Hell, could she even have driven?

But if Avery were right, that the woman welcomed the fact that he used her for sex instead of his wife, then she had no motive.

"I don't know, Jaxon," Avery said. "Joleen was really

meek around her husband. I can't imagine her standing up for me by killing him. I don't think she cared enough."

That was even sadder. "I can't believe that social worker placed you with that family."

Avery sighed. "She said she didn't have a lot of options. Joleen was right. No one wanted me and Hank, not with our father incarcerated for murder."

"Tell me about him," Jaxon said.

Bitter memories washed over her. "I was four, Hank nine. My father was upset over my mother leaving. He got in a bar fight and killed a man the same night."

"So you lost both your parents at once?"

She nodded, remembering how confused she'd been. Hank had been her rock.

But the stigma of being a jailbird kid had made her life more difficult. And then her brother had ended up in prison for homicide, as well.

Jaxon's pulse kicked up. "Did the lawyer bring up your father's history at the trial?"

Avery shrugged. "I don't remember. I wasn't in the court for the trial, just when they called me to testify."

"I'm going to study the transcripts, then talk to the prosecutor and the attorney who defended your brother. Do you remember him?"

"Not really," Avery said. "Just that he was young, a public defender."

The kid had probably been overloaded with cases, and considering Hank's confession, he hadn't dug very deep for a defense.

Jaxon turned onto the street leading to Avery's house, again struck by her home's neatly kept lawn and fresh paint. Obviously growing up in a rat trap had made her appreciate her home. "I'll let you know when I get the social worker's information and set up a time."

She handed him a business card. "You have my cell number, but this is my work number."

He glanced at it with a smile. "You work at a vet clinic?"

She nodded. "As an assistant. I like taking care of animals."

Because they gave unconditional love.

"Does that mean you have a houseful of cats?"

She gave a self-deprecating laugh. "No, no pets."

Probably went back to the attachment issue.

Amazing how easy she was to read. Yet how complicated she was at the same time. She'd lived through hell, but she'd survived and managed to make a life for herself.

"Avery, were there other foster children placed with the Mulligans when you and Hank stayed there?"

Avery rubbed her forehead in thought. "There was another girl there when we first arrived. I think her name was Lois. I'm not sure what happened to her, though."

"I'll look into it," Jaxon said. "You know, Mulligan may have abused other girls before you."

Avery's face paled. "I suppose you're right. I never really thought about it."

"It's another question for the social worker."

Anger flashed in her eyes. "Yes, it is."

He almost regretted suggesting the idea, but Avery wanted the truth, and if she hadn't been the first girl Wade had molested, the social worker might know.

Even if she hadn't known, though, another victim meant someone else had a motive to kill Wade.

"Don't think about it too much tonight," he said gently. "Just get some rest."

She reached for the door handle, then turned to face him. "Thank you again, Jaxon."

Her thanks made guilt mushroom inside him. He hadn't

done anything yet. Worse, his efforts might not make a difference at all.

Her brother could still be put to death if he didn't find some answers fast.

AVERY LET HERSELF inside her house, disturbed at the idea that Wade had hurt others before her.

And that the social worker might have known and placed her and Hank there anyway.

If Wade hadn't been murdered, he would have continued the pattern.

She wanted to thank whoever had killed him for saving future victims.

But whoever had killed him had let Hank rot in prison for his crime.

The house seemed eerily quiet tonight, making her think about Jaxon's questions. She worked at a vet clinic, but had no pets of her own. That might seem odd to him. But she'd gotten attached to a dog at one of her foster houses, and it had ripped out her heart when she'd had to leave it.

She'd vowed never to get attached to anything else again.

At the clinic, she could pet the animals, but she knew they'd be going home with their owners.

She made herself a salad, then slipped on her pajamas and turned on the television. But the news was on.

"Today, protestors against the death penalty rallied outside the prison objecting to Hank Tierney's upcoming execution."

The camera panned the crowd of protestors, who were chanting and waving signs to stop the lethal injection from happening.

Guilt plagued her for waiting so long to visit her brother. If she'd done so sooner and he'd told her the truth, she would have had more time to help him.

What if she'd waited too long and it was too late?

AVERY'S FACE HAUNTED Jaxon all night. In less than a week, her brother would be executed.

He reminded himself not to let things get personal, but he couldn't help sympathizing with her. Her eyes were like a sensual magnet drawing him to her.

He stepped onto the porch of his ranch house, pausing to listen to the creek rippling in back. He'd bought the land because he liked wide-open spaces, enjoyed riding on his days off and fishing.

Only tonight it felt quiet. Maybe too quiet. Lonely.

Hell, he liked to be alone.

But for some reason, he imagined Avery beside him, maybe sipping wine on the porch. The two of them talking in soft hushed voices. Her fingers roaming up his neck, her kisses feathering against his cheek.

Then he saw her on the ranch, riding across the pasture, her hair blowing wildly around her face. She was laughing, a musical sound that made him want to drag her off the horse and make love to her.

Dammit. He forced the images from his mind.

He had to work. Making love to Avery was not in his future.

He grabbed a beer when he went inside, dropped the take-out burger he'd picked up on his way home onto the table, then spread out the trial transcript.

The prosecuting attorney in the case was the assistant D.A. at the time, now the D.A.—Snyderman. Due to the viciousness of the attack and number of stab wounds, he'd pushed to have Hank tried as an adult. He displayed pictures of Wade Mulligan's mutilated body, showing the brutality of the crime, no doubt shocking the jurors into convicting without hesitation.

Witnesses against Hank included Avery, age nine, Joleen Mulligan, and two other foster parents, Teresa and Carl Brooks, and Philip and Sally Cotton. Both had testified that

Hank was an angry kid, that he exhibited episodes of lashing out, and that he hadn't been a good fit in their homes, that the younger children were afraid of him.

Avery's account of the events of that night read just as she'd told him. When asked if she'd been afraid of her brother, she'd said no, that he always protected her.

Neither the prosecutor nor the defense attorney had pushed her for more when they could easily have encouraged her to explain her comment. Why had Hank felt the need to protect her?

If they'd pursued that line of questioning, the truth about Wade Mulligan would at least have been exposed, garnering sympathy from the jury.

But the attorney had skimmed over the details and focused on Hank's confession.

The public defender, a new graduate barely out of diapers, had argued against the death penalty, claiming Hank was emotionally disturbed.

The A.D.A. had agreed that Hank was disturbed, but because he exhibited no signs of remorse, argued that he was psychotic. He ended his closing arguments by reminding the jurors of the number of stab wounds he'd inflicted on Wade Mulligan, arguing that Hank was not only dangerous, but also had no rehabilitative qualities.

Jaxon heaved a breath of frustration. The public defender should have requested Hank undergo a psychological exam, should have had both Hank and Avery medically evaluated and should have introduced the abuse factor. He should have researched past foster children placed with the Mulligans to see if there was a history of problems with the family.

Jaxon had hoped Casey would call with the social worker's name, but he found it in the transcripts—Delia Hanover.

According to Delia, Hank Tierney had anger issues related to his father, had trouble adapting and fitting in and he had hated Wade Mulligan. He'd asked her to move him and Avery from the home, and she was searching for another family to take them, but he killed Mulligan before she could find another placement.

Hank's attorney should have pushed her for more details on the reason Hank had requested a change.

Jaxon scrubbed his hand over the back of his neck, then sipped his beer.

At the least, the public defender should have cut a deal with the A.D.A. for an insanity plea and had Hank moved to a psychiatric hospital.

He studied the photographs of Mulligan's body, the dozens of stab wounds, and understood why the jurors had voted him guilty.

But they hadn't had all the facts.

Would these revelations be enough for a judge to grant a retrial?

He doubted it.

He needed a look at the autopsy report. But it wasn't in the file.

He would get it, though. If there were evidence of a second perpetrator, maybe that would be enough to convince a judge to stop the execution.

AVERY SHIVERED AND dug her feet into the covers. She wished she could just disappear forever.

Maybe if she pulled them up high enough over her, she could hide underneath and he wouldn't find her.

The ping, ping, ping of the rain on the tin roof sounded like nails driving down. Footsteps sounded.

Then his voice mumbling something she couldn't understand. But she knew what would come next.

"Leave her alone!" Hank shouted.

"Shut up, you little bastard."

Then a slap across the face. She'd heard the sound so

many times she should be used to it, but it still made her stomach heave.

"Beat me, but leave her alone," Hank bellowed.

Tears leaked down Avery's cheeks. Hank was always taking care of her. She clenched the sheets, sweating all over. She had to tell someone. Get her and Hank out of here.

She jumped from the bed and rushed to the door. Wade slammed his fist into Hank's stomach, but Hank lunged at him. They wrestled and fell to the floor. Hank kicked at Wade, his foot connecting with Wade's knee.

Wade grunted in pain and punched Hank again, this time so hard blood spurted from Hank's nose.

Avery covered her scream with her hand, terrified, as Wade dragged Hank to his bedroom.

He was going to tie him up. Hank wouldn't be able to help her.

She slammed her door and tried to lock it. Looked for the stick she'd sneaked into the house to try to fight him off with.

Wade shouted an obscenity, then began to pound the door with his fists. The door jarred. Wood splintered.

Avery jumped back against the wall. She was trembling all over. Felt sick to her stomach.

The door splintered and Wade stormed in. His face looked red, his eyes full of rage. He swung his hand out to grab her.

"Come here, girl. You got to earn your keep."

Avery screamed, "No," and swung the stick out. She hit him across the face, and he staggered. The rancid smell of his breath struck her as he lunged toward her and grabbed the stick.

Then he shoved her onto the bed. She looked up and saw the stick coming at her, and she covered her face with her hands and screamed again as he delivered the first blow....

Avery jerked awake, shaking all over and clawing at the bedding.

It took her a moment to realize that she was having a nightmare.

That Wade Mulligan wasn't here now, and that he could never hurt her again.

Her phone jangled, a trilling sound that sent a shiver through her. Hand trembling, she reached for it, praying Jaxon had good news.

But another voice echoed back. One that sounded garbled.

Only the words were clear.

"Your brother is a killer. He deserves to die. And you'll die, too, if you try to get him off."

Chapter Eight

Jaxon's phone buzzed, waking him at 6:00 a.m. "Sergeant Ward."

"Jaxon, it's Casey Chambers. I have some information for you."

He sat up and grabbed a pen and pad from his nightstand. "What is it?"

"I found the social worker who placed the Tierney kids with the Mulligans."

"Delia Hanover," Jaxon said. "I saw her name in the trial transcripts."

"Right," Casey said. "She left the office where she worked a couple of years after Hank Tierney was arrested. Now she works with the local school system."

"Give me her contact information."

"I'm texting you her phone and address now."

"Thanks. Anything else?"

"I did some digging around and discovered four other foster children who lived with the Mulligans before the Tierneys."

"Good work. I'd like to talk to them. Send me their names and contact information, as well."

"It's on its way. Although one of the girls, Lenny Ames, killed herself a few months after she was removed from the home."

Jaxon's heart pounded. "Is there any more information about her suicide?"

"Not much. The report was short. Said she went from the Mulligans to a juvenile center for troubled kids. She slit her wrists one night and bled out before anyone noticed."

"Did she leave a suicide note?" Jaxon asked.

"No. But the house parents at the time said she was deeply disturbed, withdrawn and depressed when she arrived."

"I suppose nobody bothered to run a psychological checkup on her?"

"Doesn't say here. But my guess is no. She was another kid who got lost in the system."

"Or died because Mulligan abused her to the point where she hadn't wanted to live anymore."

She mumbled agreement.

"Thanks, Casey. This has been very helpful."

His phone was buzzing again, another call coming in, so he pressed Connect. "Sergeant Ward."

"Jaxon, it's Avery."

Her voice sounded shaky. "What's wrong?"

"Someone just called here and threatened me."

Jaxon went still. "Stay on the line. I'll be right there." He grabbed jeans and a clean shirt and dressed quickly, stuffed his weapon in his holster and snatched his badge and Stetson.

"Do you know who the caller was?" Jaxon asked as he hurried outside to his SUV.

"No." Avery's breath rasped out. "It sounded like a man, but it was muffled, and I couldn't be sure."

"Keep the doors locked. I'll be there in a minute."

She hung up. He started the engine and drove onto the main road leading into town toward Avery's house. The sun was fighting its way through the clouds and failing, the clouds hovering above and casting a dismal gray to the land.

Avery's neighborhood was like a breath of fresh air in comparison.

But the fact that she'd been threatened made his instincts kick in, and he scanned the streets and yards in case anyone was lurking around watching her. But the street was quiet with only an occasional neighbor venturing out for the morning paper or to get in their car and head to work. Two joggers ran by, while a trio of young mothers were already strolling their babies.

Nothing suspicious.

He pulled into the driveway and parked, then hurried up to the door. Avery opened it before he could knock. "You didn't have to come," she said, although her face looked pale and she'd obviously been upset by the call. She wasn't dressed, either. She looked as if she'd hastily thrown on a robe. Her hair was tangled from sleep, her cheeks flushed.

She looked sexy as hell.

And frightened.

"Tell me exactly what happened."

She turned and walked to her kitchen. She went straight to the coffeepot, poured two cups and handed him one.

He thanked her, then blew on the steaming brew, waiting until she was ready to talk.

"I had a nightmare about Wade Mulligan," she admitted.

He gritted his teeth. Naturally asking questions about what had happened that night would stir up old nightmares for her.

"When I woke up, my phone was ringing."

"Was there a name on the caller ID?"

She shook her head. "Unknown."

"What exactly did the caller say?"

"That my brother is a killer. That he deserves to die. That I will, too, if I try to get him off."

Jaxon fisted his hands in an attempt to control his anger. Who the hell would want to scare her like that?

The only person he could think of was the person who'd killed Mulligan.

AVERY TOLD HERSELF that the call had been a prank, but still it was difficult to shake the fear that had snaked through her at the sinister words.

There had been three other calls since. All from reporters wanting an interview about her brother's upcoming execution.

"I'm going to put a tracer on your phone in case he calls back," Jaxon said.

"You think he was serious?"

Worry flashed in Jaxon's eyes a moment before he masked it. "Could be. But there are already protest rallies for both sides of the death penalty. It's possible some over-zealous fanatic is trying to scare you."

Avery's pulse began to steady. "I guess you're right. I mean, how many people even know that I'm trying to re-open the case?"

"The warden, Lisa Ellis, a social worker I asked for information, the clerk at the courthouse and Joleen Mulligan. But I can trust the social worker and clerk."

"You think Joleen would threaten me?"

"I wouldn't put it past her." Jaxon sipped his coffee. "There's another possibility."

Avery tensed at the anxiety riddling his tone. "Who?"

"The person who murdered Mulligan."

Her breath caught. "That means the threat is real."

Jaxon sighed. "I didn't mean to scare you, but we have to face the facts. If Hank didn't kill Mulligan, then who-ever did is not going to want the case reopened and another investigation."

"You're right." Avery drained the rest of her coffee and

set her cup in the sink. "But it's not going to stop me. And neither are the reporters who keep calling for interviews."

"When did that start?"

"Last week. I've refused them all, but twice I saw someone stalking me with a camera."

"Dammit. They're like vultures."

"I can handle them," Avery said. "I've been doing it all my life."

"But you shouldn't have to," Jaxon said in a voice laced with wariness and something else...maybe admiration.

No. She was reading too much into things.

Jaxon's gaze raked over her, and Avery remembered she hadn't dressed before he'd arrived. She'd been so shaken by the phone call that she'd immediately punched his number, thrown on a robe and searched the house in case whoever had phoned was inside.

"I know where Delia is," Jaxon said. "If you want to go with me, I'll wait while you dress."

Avery frowned. "You found her?"

"Yes. She left social services and is employed with the school system now."

"Does she know we're coming?"

"No. I want to surprise her."

Avery didn't bother to ask why. She didn't care. All she wanted was to hear what Delia Hanover had to say.

And if she'd had any idea what kind of people the Mulligans were before she'd sent her and Hank to live with them.

JAXON SIGHED WITH relief when Avery went to get dressed. Good grief, that thin little robe barely covered her. And that short gown showcased legs that he wanted wrapped around him.

But that was never going to happen.

The shower water kicked on, and he had to step outside for some fresh air to keep himself from thinking about how Avery would look naked with water glistening off her bronzed skin.

He had a case to solve, and the clock was ticking. He didn't have time for distractions.

Besides, Avery was not interested in him except for his expertise.

A van rolled by, slowing as it passed, and he saw someone take a picture of the house with his cell phone. Irritated, he headed toward it.

He waved at the van, and the driver pulled over to the curb. Two young men were inside, the camera guy snapping shot after shot of Avery's house and lawn.

"What are you doing?" Jaxon shouted.

The camera guy grinned. "Isn't this where the Tierney woman lives? The one whose brother's going to be executed?"

Dammit, the gawkers had already started.

"No, it's not." He flashed his badge. "What do you want with that woman anyway?"

"Just some pics. Heard she refused interviews, so I'm gonna catch her coming out and put it up on YouTube."

Then everyone would know where she lived, and all the crazies would come after her. "Get out of here, you scumbag," Jaxon said. "And if you bother Avery Tierney again, I'll arrest you for harassing innocent citizens."

The front door opened, and Avery stepped out.

"It's her!" the driver shouted. The other guy raised his camera.

Jaxon snatched the phone and deleted the pictures.

"Hey, you can't do that!" the guy shouted.

Avery apparently realized what was happening and stepped back inside the house.

"I can and I did." Jaxon shoved the phone back in the man's hands. "Now get out of here before I arrest you."

The guy cursed, but he ducked back inside the van and the driver sped off.

Jaxon waited until the van turned off the street, then went to the door.

Avery stood in the entryway, her purse slung over her shoulder.

"I'm sorry about that," he said.

Her frown deepened. "It's happened all my life. It's their last chance to get some drama out of Hank's conviction."

And make her life hell.

Avery didn't say it, but it was true. And not fair. But the media and curiosity seekers were seldom fair.

He was not going to let her be hurt by them again, though. Or by that threatening caller. He would guard her until this mess was over.

Until Hank was free and the real killer was locked behind bars.

AVERY TUGGED ON a hat as she and Jaxon left her house. She kept her head low as they drove from the neighborhood.

She'd kept to herself since she rented the house two years ago, had liked her privacy.

Publicity over the investigation and execution had robbed her of that now.

She'd considered changing her name over the years, but had decided that she wouldn't run from who she was.

By the time they arrived at the school, she'd summoned her courage. Jaxon identified himself to the receptionist in the school office.

"May I ask what this is about?" the redhead said.

"It's police business," Jaxon said.

The woman looked curious, but she refrained from pushing for more information and escorted them down the hall to the counselor's office.

She knocked on the door, then cracked it open. "Ms.

Hanover, Sergeant Jaxon Ward with the Texas Rangers is here to see you."

Jaxon stepped in, and Avery followed, twisting her hands together as she contemplated what to say. Delia Hanover was not what she'd expected or remembered. Of course, she hadn't seen her in twenty years.

Which meant Delia had been young, maybe early thirties at the time she'd known her. Her hair was slightly graying now, her eyes wary.

She rose from her desk, her face paling as her gaze latched with Avery's.

"Oh, my goodness, Avery," she rasped out. "I…guess I should have expected you to come."

Avery swallowed hard. "I saw my brother, Ms. Hanover. He's innocent."

The woman's brows pinched together. "I don't understand…"

Jaxon cleared his throat. "That's why we're here," Jaxon said. "We need your help to find the real killer, Ms. Hanover."

"Please call me Delia." She sank into her chair, a weary look in her eyes. "But Hank confessed, Avery. You said you saw him stabbing Wade Mulligan."

"Hank lied to protect me," Avery said. "He thought I stabbed Hank, so he tried to cover for me."

"Oh, my God, that can't be true," Delia said.

"I talked to him myself," Jaxon said. "And I believe his story." He planted his hands on top of her desk. "Which raises the question, who did kill Mulligan?"

The social worker's face turned ashen. "How should I know? I believed Hank."

"Think, Delia," Avery said. "Do you know anyone else who would have wanted Wade Mulligan dead?"

Chapter Nine

Jaxon studied Delia's shocked expression, searching her face for some clue that she knew more than she'd revealed. "Can you think of anyone else who would have wanted to hurt Mulligan?"

She shook her head. "No. No one that I can think of."

"What about his wife? Do you think she was capable of murdering him?"

Delia drummed her fingers on her arm. "They had their fights," she admitted. "Of course, I didn't know that when I placed Hank and Avery in the house."

"You had conducted follow-up visits to the home, didn't you?"

"A couple," Delia said, although a frown darkened her expression. "I was swamped at the time and should have gone by more often."

"Couldn't you tell that something was wrong?" He glanced at Avery and saw her bite down on her lip. "Couldn't you see the children were unhappy?"

She released a pained sigh. "None of the children I placed in foster care were happy, Sergeant Ward. Hank and Avery had already suffered the trauma and stigma of their father's arrest and their mother's abandonment. And they'd been shuffled through a half dozen other homes before I moved them to the Mulligans."

"Why were they moved from those homes?"

"Various reasons. The first family said they couldn't keep both of them. The next one, the mother had health issues. Another family claimed Hank was an angry kid and that he hit one of their own children."

"Were any other children in the Mulligan home when you placed Avery and Hank there?"

"No."

"What about Lois?" Avery asked.

Delia rubbed her forehead. "That's right. I forgot. She was there, but only about a week at the same time you were."

"What happened to her?" Jaxon asked.

Delia shrugged. "She was sent to a group home a few hours away."

"How about other children who lived with the Mulligans prior to Hank and Avery's placement?"

"I don't know much about them. I inherited the file from the former social worker, Erma Brant."

"There were no notes about abuse by the Mulligans in that file?"

Anxiety streaked Delia's face. "No. I…wish there had been."

Irritation shot through Jaxon. If she had known and had put them there anyway, she was partly responsible for what happened to Avery. "This is important, Delia. A man's life depends on it. What happened to the others?"

Delia stared at her hands, picking at her cuticles. "A couple aged out of the system. One boy was moved to a juvenile facility because he was caught stealing from a convenience store."

"Did any of the children, male or female, complain that they were abused?"

"No." She bit her nail. "And like I said, I didn't see any notes regarding abuse. I wouldn't have left Avery and Hank there if I had."

"But he abused me and my brother," Avery said. "I can't help thinking that we weren't the first."

The woman turned toward Avery, sorrow in her eyes. "I'm so sorry this happened to you, Avery. I should have seen it sooner, should have picked up on something."

"I should have told you what he was doing," Avery said. "But I was too ashamed."

"You were just a child," Delia said softly. "Mr. Mulligan was supposed to take care of you, but he took advantage of you instead."

"He said he loved me," Avery said with a bitter laugh. "That if I told anyone, he'd kill me and Hank." Her voice cracked. "It's my fault Hank went to jail. If I hadn't been so scared—"

"You had reason to be frightened." Delia walked around her desk, knelt in front of Avery and squeezed her hand. "So don't blame yourself. You were an innocent little girl, and all the adults in your life let you down. Including me." Self-recrimination underscored her voice. "If I'd known what Wade Mulligan was doing, I would have gotten you and Hank out of the house before Hank stabbed Mulligan."

Jaxon inhaled sharply. So she believed Hank was guilty. "You left your job shortly after Hank's arrest. Why did you switch jobs?"

Delia looked tormented. "Because I realized I'd made a mistake with Avery and Hank and decided I couldn't be responsible for something like that happening again."

Jaxon studied her for another long moment, then handed her a business card. "Thank you for your time. Please call me if you think of anything else that might help Hank Tierney. Especially anyone who might have had a problem with Mulligan."

She agreed, and Avery gave the woman a hug. "Thank you, Delia. Things may not have gone well at the Mulligans, but I know you tried to help me and my brother. I owe you for that."

Guilt streaked Delia's face as she hugged Avery in return. "I'm sorry about Hank. I really am."

Avery nodded, although tears filled her eyes as she pulled away.

"One more thing," Jaxon said. "Tell me the names of the other children who lived with the Mulligans."

Delia looked startled for a moment. "I'm not sure I could release that information even if I had it. But I left all those files in the social services office."

"Think about it and maybe you'll remember a name," Jaxon said. "One of them might be willing to come forward and testify about the abuse to help Hank." He pinned her with a dark look. "After all, you owe Avery and Hank that much."

AVERY STARED OUT the window at the passing scenery, Delia's ashen face flashing in her mind. Jaxon's last comment had upset the woman. But if she were upset, maybe she could help.

The bare trees looked as desolate as she felt. Hank had been in jail over half of his life and had missed the changing of the seasons, missed birthdays and holidays and building a career for himself.

She wanted him to breathe fresh air, to get a second chance at life and to spend his next birthday eating birthday cake and opening presents.

A noise sounded, and children raced onto the playground, laughing and talking. They looked so happy and carefree, just innocent kids skipping rope and playing children's games.

She and Hank had never been innocent. And neither one of them had a family.

Hank because he was incarcerated.

Her because she'd locked herself in a mental prison of her own. Shut herself off from trusting or loving a man because Mulligan had robbed her of her innocence.

She would show that bitter, mean old man that he wouldn't take anything else from her. She would get Hank out.

Then she would work on herself. Learn to trust again.

"Are you okay?" Jaxon asked as they drove away from the school.

Avery nodded. "Delia seemed sincere."

Jaxon clenched his jaw. "Maybe. But she should have pushed Hank's attorney to explore the abuse angle in Hank's defense."

Avery rubbed the scar around her wrist. "That's my fault. I should have spoken up and confided in her."

"If she was good at her job, she would have picked up on it," Jaxon said. "And she should have researched the family and made certain the home was safe and secure before leaving you there."

Avery couldn't argue with that. But she sensed Delia carried guilt around with her already regarding that mistake.

Jaxon maneuvered through traffic until he reached the body shop on the edge of town. Several rusted, broken-down cars sat on cinder blocks, a fenced-in area held a mountain of old tires and other car parts and pieces, ranging from new fenders to motors, were scattered across the junkyard.

"What are we doing here?" Avery asked.

"Casey, my contact at the social service office, sent me a list of children who lived with the Mulligans prior to you and your brother. One of the boys, Shane Fowler, runs this place."

Avery's heart pounded. "You think if we get some of the others to speak up, it might help Hank."

Jaxon frowned and adjusted his hat as he reached for the

door handle. "It might. It'll certainly establish a pattern of abuse, which could be argued in a self-defense plea."

Hope fluttered in Avery's chest. Mulligan had abused her and Hank.

Which meant they most likely weren't the first. And they probably wouldn't have been the last if someone hadn't stopped the old man by ending his life.

THE JUNKYARD LOOKED like a sad place where old cars had gone to die. Jaxon had worked at one when he was a teenager, though, and he understood the value of recycling, of reusing good parts in another vehicle to save the owner the cost of expensive repairs.

He also couldn't fault any guy from making an honest living, and being an auto mechanic or specializing in body repairs took skills.

Ironically, though, Mulligan had worked at a garage years ago.

Jaxon took Avery's elbow as they walked across the yard to the office. Hubcaps, tires and an assortment of axels were scattered in organized piles near the trailer. He knocked but no one answered, so he opened the door and peeked inside.

"No one is here."

Avery touched his arm. "I see someone over there."

She pointed to a row lined with hoods, and Jaxon headed that way. "Mr. Fowler?"

A stocky man wearing a plaid shirt and overalls looked up, adjusted his hat to shade his eyes and frowned. His arms were tatted up, a jagged scar discolored his left cheek and his hands looked battered and bruised. "Yeah?"

Jaxon flashed his badge, identified himself and introduced Avery.

"Am I in some sort of trouble with the law?" Fowler coughed into his hand. "I mean, I pay my taxes and all. And I run a legitimate business."

The man's paranoia made Jaxon question whether or not he might be doing something illegal. But Jaxon wasn't interested in petty crimes.

"No, sir," Jaxon said. "We came to talk to you about Wade Mulligan. You lived with him when you were a kid, didn't you?"

Fowler's eyes sharpened. "Yeah. But that was a lifetime ago."

Avery cleared her throat. "Shane, I'm Hank Tierney's sister, Avery. We also lived with the Mulligans."

"Aw, hell," the man muttered. "I shoulda recognized you from the news. They been talking about your brother's execution all week. Showed a picture of you when you was little."

Avery's mouth twitched. "That's because the date is approaching. I'm trying to stop him from being put to death."

Fowler wiped his greasy hands on a rag he pulled from his back pocket. "What's that got to do with me?"

"Both Hank and Avery were abused by Mr. Mulligan." Jaxon watched for a reaction, but Fowler didn't seem surprised. "How was the family when you lived with the Mulligans?"

The man backed up, his posture defensive. "Like I said, it was a long damn time ago."

"But you remember whether or not he hit you," Jaxon said.

Fowler ran a hand across the scar on his face. "So what if he did? I was a smart mouth back then."

"Were there any girls living in the home when you lived there?" Jaxon asked.

Fear flickered in Fowler's gray eyes. "Yeah, a couple."

"Did Wade Mulligan ever go in their room at night?"

Fowler rubbed his hands on the grease rag again, looking into the black smears as if they might offer him a way out.

"I was just a kid back then," he said. "I didn't know what he was doing was wrong."

Avery sucked in a sharp breath. "So he did molest the girls?"

Fowler looked up at her, guilt registering a second before he jerked his head to stare across his junkyard. "I didn't see nothing, but I heard 'em crying at night. I went to the door once, but he beat me and told me to stay out of grown-up business."

"So you stayed quiet?" Jaxon said, unable to hide the disgust in his tone.

Fowler gestured toward his scarred cheek. "Monster sliced my face that night. Said the next time he'd put that knife in my gut. What the hell was I supposed to do?"

"You could have told someone," Avery said angrily. "You could have called 911 or let the social worker know. If you had, you might have saved those girls and me and my brother."

AVERY WAS TREMBLING so badly she thought she was going to have to sit down. Anger at this man ballooned inside her. If he'd turned in Mulligan, she and Hank would have been spared.

Their entire life had been destroyed by the events that had happened in that house. Events that could have been prevented.

"I'm sorry," Fowler said, his voice almost childlike now. "I was scared. I…know I shoulda said something."

"Classic abuse," Jaxon said. "Who were the girls who were there when you were?"

Fowler leaned against the fence, wiping sweat from his neck with his hand. "Priscilla Janice and Renee Feldon."

"Do you know where either of them are now?"

"Priscilla OD'd on heroin a few years back. Don't know

where Renee is. Last I heard she was turning tricks on the streets."

"When was that?" Jaxon asked.

"About ten years ago."

Avery clenched her hands together. One girl had overdosed while another resorted to hooking. No doubt both their problems had been caused by Wade Mulligan's abuse.

"If we get a stay for Hank Tierney, would you be willing to testify to the abuse?" Jaxon asked.

Fowler looked down at his shoes. "I don't know. I'm not sorry the bastard's dead, but I ain't proud that he used me for a punching bag."

"Please," Avery said. "Wade Mulligan deserved to die, but my brother didn't kill him."

Jaxon cleared his throat. "You want your self-respect back? Then stand up to him."

"But he's dead," Fowler said.

"My brother isn't," Avery said quietly.

The man looked up at her, his scar reddening in the sunlight. "All right, I'll do it."

They thanked him, then walked back to the car in silence. Avery flipped on the radio to distract herself from the bitterness eating at her as Jaxon drove from the parking lot.

But a special newscast was airing. "This late-breaking story in. Hank Tierney, whose execution is scheduled just a few days away, was stabbed today in a prison fight. Guards were moving him from his cell block when a fire erupted in a neighboring cell. Before they realized what was happening, two inmates attacked Tierney."

Avery choked on a sob while she waited to hear if her brother was still alive.

Chapter Ten

"Tierney was taken to the infirmary, where he was treated and received thirteen stitches in his abdomen," the reporter continued. "Investigators are looking into the attack, and Tierney has been moved to isolation for his protection."

Avery clutched her middle, pain knifing through her. "I have to go see him."

"I doubt they'll allow that," Jaxon said. "But I can call and make sure he's all right."

"Will you?"

"Of course." He was beginning to think he'd do anything she asked. He retrieved his cell phone and punched the number for the prison. "Yes, this is Sergeant Jaxon Ward. I need to speak to the warden."

A pause, and then Jaxon spoke again.

"I'm calling to check on Hank Tierney."

Silence from Jaxon while he listened to the warden, then a heavy sigh. "All right, alert me if there are any more problems."

Avery tugged at his arm as he hung up. "Well, how is he?"

"No major organs were damaged. He's going to be all right."

His comment didn't soothe her worries. "Why would someone attack Hank?"

Jaxon squared his shoulders. "Prison fights are almost a daily occurrence, Avery. You can't read too much into this."

Avery's anger rose. "The timing has to mean something. Somebody wants Hank dead." She clutched Jaxon's arm, the wheels turning in her head. "Do you think it's because we're asking questions?"

Jaxon's hands tightened around the steering wheel. "That's possible, but it might not be related to us. Hank probably made enemies on the inside."

"But why try to kill him when he's scheduled to die?" Emotions clogged Avery's throat. "The only answer that makes sense is that someone doesn't want him to be cleared."

Jaxon cut his eyes toward her, his expression dark. "Try not to jump to conclusions, Avery."

"How can I not?" Hysteria clawed at her. "First I receive a threatening call and now Hank is attacked."

Jaxon cupped her face between his hands. "Look at me, Avery. Hank is going to be all right. And I'm not going to let anyone hurt you."

She blinked to stem the tears, but she was terrified for Hank and for herself.

Maybe Hank had survived this time, but what if someone came after him again?

UNABLE TO STAND to see Avery suffering, Jaxon pulled her into his arms and rubbed her back. "I'm sorry, Avery. You don't deserve this."

"Maybe I do," she said in a low voice. "If I hadn't told the police I saw Hank stabbing Wade, maybe the lawyers would have gotten him off."

"It's not your fault," Jaxon said. "There was too much evidence against Hank anyway. Even without his confession, his prints on the knife and the number of stab wounds would have earned him a conviction." She relaxed against him for a moment, and he stroked her hair. The sweet scent of her fruity shampoo suffused him, stirring emotions and desires he didn't want to feel.

She was strong and resilient, but she had deserved to have adults who loved her and took care of her, not ones who mistreated her and made her feel ashamed.

Answering her questions about the attack on her brother wasn't simple, either. It was very possible that Hank was assaulted because they were trying to free him.

There were protestors both for and against his execution. The story had been splattered across the news for the past two weeks. And if one of the other kids who'd lived with Mulligan had killed him, that person wouldn't want Hank exonerated and the finger pointed at him or her.

"But Hank's been through so much," she said. "I hate to think about him being in solitary confinement."

"It's for his protection," Jaxon said. "Now, there's another foster child who lived with the Mulligans that we need to question."

Avery sighed against him and lifted her head. Her eyes were luminous with pain and something else indefinable. Maybe surprise that she'd allowed herself to lean on him.

She inhaled sharply, visibly pulling herself together. "Who is it?"

Jaxon released her, instantly missing the feel of her in his arms. "Lois Thacker, the girl you remembered. She's a cop."

Avery's eyes flickered with a spark of hope. "Let's go."

Jaxon started the engine and swung the vehicle back onto the road. Avery turned to look out the window while he drove toward Laredo.

AVERY CLOSED HER eyes during the ride and fell asleep, her mind heavy with fear for Hank and the pressing time restraints of getting him released.

But her nightmares returned to another night at the Mulligans....

It was dark inside, the rain pinging off the tin roof. Joleen was passed out on the couch, and Wade had just come in. He saw there was no food on the table and bellowed, then threw the cast-iron skillet across the room. It hit the wall with a bang, then dropped to the floor with a thunderous sound.

"Come on, Avery." Hank grabbed her hand and they ran outside. Rain soaked them, but they didn't stop running until they reached the old shed. Hank slid open the door and ushered her inside.

"We'll hide behind that cabinet." They crawled behind the cabinet, pulling an old blanket over them to hide in case Wade came looking.

A few minutes later, the door screeched open. Then Wade yelled their names. A cigarette lighter flicked, the glow of it bursting into the shed.

She buried her head against her brother, and he covered her with himself as they waited in the dark....

Avery jerked awake as the car stopped, trembling as she recalled what had happened next. In a fit of rage, Wade had thrown tools and junk across the shed.

But he hadn't found them.

They'd spent the night there that evening, cowering and hiding and cold.

Hank had saved her.

She had to save him now.

When she looked up, Jaxon was watching her. "Bad dream?"

Embarrassed, she looked down at her hands. At the scar that was always there, reminding her of where she'd come from. Not that she needed it.

Her scars ran deep.

"Memories."

His dark gaze settled over her, and he reached out and covered her hand with his. She started to pull away, but he touched the scar with one finger, and she watched him trace it.

"We'll get the truth, Avery. I promise."

She wanted to curl her hand in his as she had done with Hank's when she was small. Wanted to bury herself against him and hold on to him forever.

But she had to stand on her own.

JAXON AND AVERY stopped at the receptionist desk, where he introduced himself and Avery and asked to speak to Lois Thacker. He'd already looked her up and learned she was a beat cop and covered a section of town known for hookers, addicts and the homeless.

"She and her partner, Bain Whitefeather, are on patrol now."

"Can you call her and ask her to meet us?" Jaxon said.

The woman nodded, made the call, then hung up. "She said to meet her at the Cactus Coffee Shop."

"Thanks." He and Avery walked back outside to his SUV, and he plugged the name of the coffee shop into his GPS. Fifteen minutes later, they parked in front of the small corner café with the big cactus in front. A patrol car sat next to the sign, a Native American cop inside on the radio.

When they entered, he spotted a female in uniform already seated with coffee in a booth. She was probably in her mid-thirties, with dirty blond hair, a sharp angled face and short wide hands. She was slightly overweight, wore no makeup and her curly hair was cropped short.

"Do you want something?" he asked Avery.

"Just plain coffee."

He ordered them each a cup, and then they walked over to Lois. He flashed his badge and identified himself.

Avery extended her hand. "I'm Avery Tierney. Thank you for meeting us, Lois."

The cop's gray eyes flickered with recognition. "You're Hank Tierney's sister?"

Avery nodded, her body tense. "His execution is coming up, and I'm trying to stop it."

"Hmm. Interesting." Lois rubbed her hand over the baton at her waist. "I thought he did it. In fact, I was tempted to send him a thank-you note. Can't believe they convicted him in the first place."

"I agree," Avery said.

Jaxon adjusted his Stetson. "We now have reason to believe he didn't murder Mulligan, that his confession was false."

Lois pursed her thick lips. "False? Only time that happens is when a suspect is coerced or covering for someone else." Her gaze latched on to Avery. "That it? He covered for you?"

"Yes, because he thought I stabbed Wade Mulligan, but I didn't."

"We think that someone else came into the house that night and killed Mulligan," Jaxon explained. "So we're talking to everyone associated with the Mulligan family."

"The old lady hated him," Lois admitted. "But she was scared to death of him, too. I can't imagine her having the guts to stab him." She shrugged. "Although from what I've seen on the streets, you never know about people. She could have had it planned and sneaked in and offed him."

"How long did you live with the Mulligans?" Jaxon asked.

Lois scowled and then took a swig of her coffee. "About a year. I was thirteen at the time."

Jaxon's pulse spiked. "Thirteen. Were any other kids there when you lived in the house?"

Anger tightened the lines on Lois's face. "Yeah. A little girl named Dotty."

"What happened when you were at the house?" Jaxon asked.

Lois clenched the coffee cup so tightly coffee spilled over. "Joleen drank a lot, passed out almost every night."

Avery cleared her throat. "And Wade?"

Lois looked up at Avery, pain mingling with rage. "He used to come in my room. Used me. Hit me. Did whatever he wanted while Joleen lay passed out in the other room."

"Did you ever tell anyone?" he asked.

She rubbed a hand down her coffee cup. "Not at first. I tried to fight him off, but I was a scrawny thing back then. Didn't do any good."

"So he continued?" Avery said.

Lois nodded. "But one night when he was done with me, I heard him going into Dotty's room." Her voice warbled. "She was seven. The tiniest little thing you ever saw. Scared of the dark and dogs and everything else in the world."

Silence stretched between them, the reality needling Jaxon. "What happened that night?"

"I grabbed the baseball bat, ran in there and hit the bastard with it. Knocked him upside the head till he got off Dotty."

Pain wrenched Avery's face, making Jaxon want to hold her again. But they had to finish this interview.

"Next day the old man sent me away. But I was scared for Dotty and told the social worker what happened."

Avery gasped softly "You told on him?"

Lois nodded, her eyes grave with dark memories. "Heard they took Dotty to another house. I thought they might lock the old man up, but they didn't." She tapped her badge. "That's when I decided to become a cop. Try to clean garbage off the streets."

"Do you know what happened to Dotty?" Jaxon asked.

Lois propped her head on one hand for a moment, then gave a clipped nod. "Used my connections here at the department about a year ago and found out that she died in an alley. Pimp beat her to death."

Avery gasped. "That's horrible."

"What's bad is that I tried to help Dotty by telling, and

it didn't do a damn bit of good. Two months after I was taken away, I heard they were putting kids back with the Mulligans."

"Who was the social worker?" Jaxon asked.

"Some lady named Erma Brant."

"She never should have placed other kids there," Avery whispered.

Jaxon nodded agreement as he studied Lois. She'd been abused by the old man, caught him abusing another younger girl, then been removed from the home. She must have been furious when she learned more children were being put in that situation.

Had she been angry enough to sneak back to the Mulligans' and kill Wade, then escape without anyone knowing she was there?

Chapter Eleven

Jaxon studied Lois. She was tough, strong, had been a fighter. And she was smart.

Smart enough to have planned revenge on Mulligan?

"Lois, where were you the night Mulligan was murdered?"

Lois's sharp gaze flew to Jaxon, her jaw twitching. "Damn. You think I killed the old man?"

Jaxon shrugged. "If Hank didn't, it stands to reason that one of the other kids who'd been abused by him did."

Lois ran a finger along the rim of her cup. "I suppose I can see why you'd think that." She scribbled down a number and a name. "The night he died, I was at a group home. The house parent's name was Henrietta."

"Does she still live there?" Jaxon asked.

"Yeah, I had to see a juvy there about a month ago. Place hasn't changed a bit. Old and run-down, but Henrietta was decent. If it wasn't for her, I might have wound up on the streets."

Avery shifted in her chair. "Can you think of anyone else who would have wanted Wade dead? Another kid who was placed there?"

"Hell, probably all of them."

True, Jaxon thought. "Anyone specific?"

The cop finished her coffee and crumpled the cup in her

hands. "There was one other boy and his sister who lived with the Mulligans before me. I heard Mulligan used to beat the boy, and later, that his sister got pregnant."

Suspicions mounted in Jaxon's mind. "What happened?"

"Mulligan forced the girl to get an abortion. I think she wound up having a breakdown or something."

"Did Erma Brant place them there, as well?"

Lois nodded. "If you ask me, that woman should have had to serve time herself."

THIRTY MINUTES LATER, Avery and Jaxon located BJ Wilson at a rehab facility on the east side of town. The way the rustic building was set back on farmland and surrounded by trees made it look like a wilderness retreat.

A barn looked as if it held horses, and another area appeared to be used for farming. Part of the therapy for the residents?

From Jaxon's phone call, he'd learned BJ was a heroin addict and had been caught stealing from his employer.

He'd spent two years in prison, but upon release, he immediately hit the streets for drugs. According to his probation officer, he'd managed to get BJ in rehab instead of sending him back to prison, but he wasn't hopeful the guy would last.

"I feel sorry for him," Avery said as they entered the rehab clinic. "No doubt his past put him here."

"Choices put him here," Jaxon said in a brusque tone. "A lot of people experience trauma in their lives. Not everyone turns to drugs or violence to deal with it."

"But he never had a chance."

Jaxon shrugged. "You went through hell, but you didn't turn to drugs or violence."

Avery's heart swelled at the admiration in his tone. Then again, he was giving her too much credit. She might not be an addict or a criminal, but she was scarred.

She'd never had a relationship with a man in her life. Never gotten close to anyone.

A receptionist greeted them and showed them to the director's office. On both sides of the hall were rooms that resembled classrooms, and a medical office sat on the corner of the corridor. Another door led to an outside garden area, complete with a recreational area that included seating, card tables, an area for arts and crafts activities and a path that looked as if it led to the creek.

The director, Cam Sanders, was a middle-aged woman with wavy red hair and a kind smile but sad eyes.

Jaxon introduced himself and Avery and explained that he needed to talk to BJ.

"How is he doing?" Avery asked.

"He's been here three weeks and finally settling in. But I'm not sure he'll make it out on the streets by himself. He needs supervision and structure and doesn't seem to be able to manage that on his own."

She steepled her hands on the desk. "What is it you want to talk to him about?"

Avery glanced at Jaxon, and he indicated for her to take the lead.

"My brother is Hank Tierney." She paused, giving Ms. Sanders time to process her statement. Recognition quickly dawned.

"I see. What do you and your brother have to do with BJ?"

"We lived in the same foster home, not at the same time, but BJ knew the man my brother was accused of killing."

"Other than dredging up painful memories, what do you think you'll accomplish by talking to BJ?"

Jaxon shifted. "We're building a case to show that Wade Mulligan was abusive to the children under his care."

The director buttoned her suit coat. "But Hank Tierney

confessed, and proving Mulligan was abusive only confirms his motive."

"Yes, but it also opens the door to others with motive, which could be enough to cast reasonable doubt on Hank," Jaxon pointed out.

Irritation flashed in the woman's eyes. "So you came here to ask BJ if he killed Mulligan?"

Avery's stomach clenched. "No. We just want to know what happened with him and his sister."

Ms. Sanders stood. "I don't know if that's a good idea. The counselor working with him said his traumatic past contributed to his addiction problems."

"My brother's life depends on us learning the truth," Avery argued.

Jaxon crossed his arms. "Isn't facing the truth imperative for a patient's recovery?"

Ms. Sanders worried her bottom lip with her teeth, fidgeting as if she were debating the issue. "Let me speak to BJ's counselor. If he agrees, I'll let you talk to him."

"Thank you," Avery and Jaxon both murmured at once.

The woman's heels clicked as she crossed the room and left. Jaxon paced to the window and looked out. The skies looked gloomy and gray, winter taking its toll as wind swirled dead grass and tumbleweed across the parking lot.

A second later, the director returned. "All right. Dr. Kemp says you can speak with BJ, but only in his presence."

They followed the woman down a hall past several private rooms to a sunroom off the back that overlooked the creek.

A thin man in his late thirties wearing jeans and a flannel shirt sat in a straight chair at a small table set up with checkers. He looked antsy and nervous and kept tapping one of the checkers against the board.

Another man, more distinguished looking, graying at his temples, sat across from him. Obviously the therapist. He angled himself toward them as they approached.

Ms. Sanders introduced them, and Dr. Kemp gestured for them to join him and BJ around the checkers table. The doctor addressed BJ. "BJ, Jaxon Ward is a Texas Ranger, and Avery's brother, Hank, is in prison for murdering Wade Mulligan."

BJ rocked himself back and forth, his eyes twitching as if he had a nervous tic.

"You… Hank killed him. That's good," BJ said.

Avery sucked in a deep breath. "Wade Mulligan deserved to die, didn't he, BJ?"

BJ clawed at his arms. "Yeah, he was a monster."

"Did he hurt you and your sister?" Jaxon asked.

BJ clawed harder, drawing Avery's gaze to his track marks. "Yeah, he was mean. He used to beat me. And what he did to Imogene… I should have killed him."

Avery's heart pounded, but Dr. Kemp gave her a warning look.

"Did she tell anyone what he did?" Jaxon asked.

Emotions clouded BJ's face, his eyes twitching again. "No, she was ashamed. But she cried all the time and then she got pregnant."

"I'm so sorry for what he did," Avery said. "I know how she felt, how you felt, because Wade Mulligan did the same thing to me and my brother."

"He got you pregnant?" BJ asked.

Avery quickly shook her head. "No, but he came into my room at night. I used to cry all the time, too. And I was glad when he died."

"Me, too." BJ stood and bounced from one foot to the other. "I wanted to kill him. I should have. Especially after he made Imogene get rid of the baby." His voice cracked. "That destroyed her. She didn't want to be pregnant, but she hated what he made her do. And then she got so depressed she cut her wrists with a kitchen knife."

Avery's breath grew pained as she imagined the scene.

"Did you see her do that?" she asked softly.

BJ stopped bouncing and sank into his chair again, then looked at the doctor.

"Go on, BJ, you're doing fine," Dr. Kemp encouraged.

BJ wiped at his eyes. "No, but I found her. She climbed in the bathtub. She wasn't naked or anything. She was just in there in her clothes, and she cut her wrists and there was blood everywhere." He sniffed and rubbed his nose on his sleeve. "I guess she got in the tub 'cause she knew he'd be mad if she made a mess on the floor."

Tears burned the backs of Avery's eyelids. If Imogene had attempted suicide in that house, why had the social worker placed her and Hank there afterward?

JAXON GRITTED HIS teeth at the injustice of the entire situation. People hadn't been doing their jobs, or else so many kids wouldn't have been hurt by Mulligan.

He wanted to have a chat with Erma Brant.

But he forced his voice to be calm when he addressed BJ. "What happened after the suicide attempt?"

BJ looked to the doctor as if asking permission to finish, and Dr. Kemp gave him an encouraging nod. "They took her to a hospital," BJ said. "And from there to a juvenile facility. They tried to put me in a group home, but after the Mulligans, I wasn't going to stay, so I ran away."

"Where did you go?" Avery asked.

"I lived on the streets." BJ shrugged as if that had been nothing. "It was better than getting beat every day and watching your sister get molested."

"Where's your sister now?" Avery asked.

BJ became agitated again and clawed at his arms once more. "In a hospital. They say she went crazy. Half the time, she doesn't even know me anymore."

His voice choked, and Dr. Kemp stood and rubbed BJ's shoulders. "You did good, BJ. I know it's painful, but remember what we said about healing. Talking about it can help."

"How?" he cried. "It doesn't change a damn thing. Imogene's still locked up in that crazy house." He flung his hand across the checkers and sent them scattering across the floor. "And look at me. I'm nothing but a junkie."

"You're stronger than you think," Dr. Kemp said. "You're working hard in therapy and on your way to recovery."

Jaxon sensed it was time to leave, but he had to ask one more question. "Where were you the night Mulligan was killed, BJ?"

Dr. Kemp pivoted, eyes blazing with anger.

BJ looked stunned for a moment as if he didn't understand the question.

"That's enough," Dr. Kemp said. "We're finished."

Jaxon watched BJ sink into the chair and begin rocking himself again. "Do you remember, BJ?"

BJ's eyes looked tormented as he lifted his head. "I told you, on the streets. Probably passed out in a ditch somewhere."

Dr. Kemp gestured toward the door. "I said, it's time to go."

Jaxon gave him a clipped nod, then placed his hand at the back of Avery's waist. "Thank you for talking to us, BJ."

Avery didn't speak as they walked out to the car, but once they shut the door, she sagged against the seat. "I feel so bad for him and his sister."

Jaxon nodded. "So do I. But remember, Avery. If Hank didn't kill Mulligan, someone else did."

Her eyes widened. "You think BJ might have?"

He shrugged and started the engine. "Both he and Imogene had motive. And he has no alibi."

Avery fiddled with her jacket. "You're right. He could have been high, killed Wade and not even remembered it."

Jaxon clenched the steering wheel with a white-knuckled

grip. "True. And it'll be hard to prove, although his story could cast doubt on Hank's guilt." He pulled out of the parking lot. "There's one more thing. BJ said his sister tried to kill herself with a kitchen knife. Mulligan was also stabbed with a kitchen knife."

"That's right," Avery said. "Hank admitted he took a knife from the kitchen earlier that day."

"According to the trial transcript, the prosecutor argued that act implied the murder was premeditated."

"He took it to defend himself and me," Avery interjected.

"I understand that," Jaxon said. "And I don't blame Hank. I wouldn't blame BJ or Imogene or Lois Thacker, either, if they'd killed Mulligan. I just don't understand why the defense attorney didn't bring all this up at the trial."

"Because of the confession," Avery admitted, her voice heavy.

"It was still shoddy police work and defense work," Jaxon said. "Let's talk to Imogene and see if she can add anything to BJ's story. Then we'll pay Hank's original attorney a visit. And we're going to talk to Erma Brant."

"I have some questions for her," Avery said darkly.

He spun the vehicle toward the local psychiatric hospital. If Imogene were as unstable as BJ implied, they might not learn anything.

Then again, with every person who confirmed that Mulligan was an abuser and rapist, they added another suspect to the growing list.

Suspects that might lead them to the real killer. Or at least to a new trial that could save Hank's life.

"AVERY TIERNEY IS working with a Texas Ranger to get her brother exonerated."

"But Hank stabbed Mulligan a dozen times."

"True. But the Ranger says he only confessed to save his sister because he thought she killed Mulligan."

That statement could blow the original case to hell.

No...it was the pathetic attempt of a death row inmate to save himself at the last minute, nothing more.

But if a Ranger was asking questions and got a new trial, police would be looking for the real killer.

That would be dangerous.

Hell, Hank Tierney had been violent and had stabbed his foster father multiple times. That was the damn truth.

Whether or not he'd delivered the deadly blow didn't matter, did it?

Hank was violent. He would have hurt someone else. Probably *would* have killed someone if he hadn't been stopped.

Getting him off the streets had been the best thing for everyone, hadn't it?

Chapter Twelve

Avery had been surprised the rehab facility wasn't drab and depressing. Instead the sunroom and outside facilities were cheery and relaxing.

But the mental hospital radiated a different feel. The building was housed behind a gate, as if it were a prison. The building was old and weathered, the land dry and parched. Jaxon phoned ahead to ask permission to visit Imogene, and was given an okay, although the nurse in charge warned him that Imogene would probably be unresponsive.

Inside, the hospital walls were painted a dull green, the floors were faded gray and everything from the dingy chairs in the waiting room to the cafeteria they passed desperately need a face-lift.

The doctor in charge of Imogene's care, a fiftysomething bohemian-looking lady, met them in her office. "I'm Dr. Pirkle. I understand the reason you're here, but I'm not sure Imogene will be helpful."

"Just let us talk to her for a minute," Jaxon said. "It's important."

The woman's sharp eyes darted sideways to Avery. "Her mental state is fragile. She's making strides, but she suffered a psychotic break, is bipolar and struggles with depression. She doesn't need a setback."

"We don't want to hurt her," Avery said. "You can be

present when we talk to her. And the moment you sense we might be upsetting her, we'll leave."

Dr. Pirkle stood, her brows knitted. "All right. Follow me."

She led them to a room across from another nurse's station. Dr. Pirkle knocked gently on the door and opened it.

Avery's heart hammered at the sight of the frail-looking blonde sitting by the window staring outside. She was so thin that Avery wondered if she ever ate, her skin so pale she obviously didn't get out in the sun much.

She didn't look at them as they crossed the room, but kept her hands buried in the folds of the blanket on her lap. Unlike her brother, whose anxiety had displayed itself by perpetual motion, Imogene was so still she might have been a stone statue.

Dr. Pirkle laid a hand on Imogene's shoulder and knelt in front of her. "Imogene, you have some visitors." She introduced them, but Imogene didn't show a reaction.

The doctor stood and gestured for them to begin.

"Why don't you try talking to her?" Jaxon suggested to Avery.

Emotion thickened her throat as she pulled a chair from the corner and situated it beside Imogene. When she sat down, she offered Imogene a smile.

"Imogene, I'm Avery," she said softly. "We just talked to your brother, BJ."

Her eyelids fluttered, and she slowly turned her head to look at her. Avery's chest constricted at the flat, dead look in the young woman's eyes.

"He's all right," Avery said. "He loves you and misses you, Imogene."

Imogene's lip quivered slightly.

"He's sorry that you're having a hard time and wants you to get better."

Imogene's breath quickened slightly.

"I know what happened to you," Avery said softly. "Because I lived in the house with Wade and Joleen Mulligan."

Tension stretched in the silence, Imogene's breath becoming unsteady.

"Mr. Mulligan hurt me, too," Avery said. "And my brother, Hank, he used to beat him like he did your brother."

Imogene's hands dug deeper into the blanket.

"One night after Mr. Mulligan came into my room, he ended up dead. The police thought my brother killed him. You may have heard the story."

Imogene looked into Avery's eyes, her only acknowledgment.

"But they were wrong. Hank did stab Wade, but Wade was already dead." She paused, searching for a reaction.

An odd, eerie smile slowly formed on Imogene's face.

"We believe someone else sneaked into the house that night. Someone who took a kitchen knife and stabbed Wade before my brother came into the room."

"You and your brother had reason to hate Mulligan," Jaxon said. "He forced you to have an abortion. Your brother ran away and started doing drugs."

"Do you think it's possible that he broke into the house and killed Wade?" Avery asked.

Dr. Pirkle's soft gasp of disapproval echoed between them.

"I did it," Imogene said, shocking them all. "I wanted him dead."

Her eyes suddenly looked wild, excited, crazed. She lifted her hands above her head, positioning them as if she were holding a knife, and brought it down in a stabbing motion. "I hated him and wanted him dead. I stabbed him in the chest, over and over and over." Her voice rose, her breath raspy as she continued the motion. "He shouted out in pain, but this time I was the one making him cry. He begged me to stop, begged me to let him go, but I didn't." She shook her head back and forth, lost in the moment. "I stabbed him again. Blood spurted everywhere. All over his chest and face, all over my hands." She looked down and touched her shirt. "All over my blouse. I had a white blouse on that day, but then it was red. But it looked pretty that way. Pretty with his blood on it because that meant he was dead, and he couldn't ever touch me again."

She drove her hands down one more time, twisting them around and around as if she were burying the knife inside Wade Mulligan's body. "And then he stopped crying. Stopped breathing. It was so beautiful."

Another silence fell over the room as they digested what she'd said.

"So you killed Wade Mulligan?" Jaxon finally asked.

Dr. Pirkle cleared her throat. "That's enough."

Imogene closed her eyes and made a soft mewling sound. "I killed him. Then BJ killed him again. Then we dragged his body outside and dug a hole and buried him in it. I threw dirt on his face and laughed and laughed and laughed as we spread it over him. Then BJ pried open his mouth and dumped more dirt inside it so he couldn't ever yell or say vile things again." She started to hum beneath her breath. "We covered him all over so we'd never see those mean eyes again, never see them again...."

Avery's stomach knotted.

Had Imogene or her brother really stabbed Wade, or was she simply delusional?

JAXON AND AVERY waited in the hallway for Dr. Pirkle as she spoke to Imogene. When she emerged from the room, anger slashed her features.

"I can't believe you came here to implicate Imogene in a crime to exonerate your brother, Miss Tierney." She slanted Jaxon a harsh look. "And you, Sergeant Ward, you know that anything Imogene said in her condition is not going to stand up in court."

"I'm aware of that," Jaxon said. "But if Imogene did kill Mulligan, or if her brother did, and you know the truth, you should tell us."

"Anything I've learned through my patient's private therapy sessions is privileged and you know that, too."

Avery sighed next to him, and Jaxon wanted to pull her up against him, but he refrained. "Yes, of course. Although if Imogene killed Wade, you could use an insanity defense. And Hank would get the freedom he deserves."

"She didn't kill him," Dr. Pirkle said. "Although she certainly sounded venomous in there, her story was just that—a story. A fantasy. In her delusions, she has imagined doing what she didn't have the courage to do back then."

"You mean she blames herself?" Avery asked.

Dr. Pirkle shrugged. "Most victims experience some sort of self-blame, think they deserved the abuse and ask themselves why they didn't do things differently." Her stare pierced Avery. "I'm sure you understand that feeling."

Jaxon's jaw tightened, but Avery simply nodded.

"More than you know." She lifted her chin. "That's one reason I'm determined to free my brother. He wouldn't have lied about killing Wade if he hadn't been protecting me."

Dr. Pirkle squeezed Avery's hand in hers. "I'm truly sorry for how you've suffered, for how your brother suffered. After hearing Imogene's story, I believe that man deserved what he got. But I don't see how I can help you any further."

Jaxon wanted to be angry with the doctor, but he understood her position. Hell, Imogene was an emotionally unstable woman and needed protection.

But he hadn't learned anything new here, and he needed something that would make a judge grant a stay for Hank.

He thanked Dr. Pirkle, and he and Avery walked down the hall, the silence thick with anxiety.

His phone buzzed, and he checked the text. The forensic examiner from the lab.

Stop by. I need to show you something I saw on Mulligan's autopsy report.

Jaxon texted that he'd be right there, then gestured for Avery to get in the SUV.

"We're going to the lab," Jaxon said. "Our analyst finally reviewed Mulligan's autopsy."

Avery leaned against the back of the seat, a troubled look on her face. "Imogene is a wreck and her brother an addict. I'm not sure they can help us.'

"Two more lives completely destroyed by Wade Mulligan," Jaxon muttered.

"I know. Which makes me wonder why the social worker placed me and Hank with the family. I can't believe nobody picked up on the problems in that house. Especially after Lois and Dotty."

"Someone should have stopped him," Jaxon agreed. "We're going to talk to Erma Brant after we see this autopsy and find out just what she was thinking."

Avery twisted her hands together. "How does she live with herself?"

"Good question. Ask her that when we see her."

"I intend to."

Dark clouds hovered above, threatening rain, late-afternoon shadows slanting across the road. It took almost an hour to reach the county lab, which was housed in an old brick building, set away from the road about a mile from the warehouse district.

They bypassed several offices and labs where workers were processing evidence collected from various cases, running DNA tests and analyzing photographs.

Jaxon knocked on the door to Dr. Jeremy Riggins's office. The doctor yelled for him to come in, and Avery followed him inside. Jaxon made the introductions, and Dr. Riggins led them over to his workstation.

"I studied the autopsy report," Dr. Riggins said. "Wade Mulligan definitely bled out from a stab wound that penetrated his aorta."

That was nothing new.

"You said you found something else?" Jaxon asked.

Dr. Riggins glanced at Avery. "Maybe you should step out, Miss Tierney. What I'm going to show you is pretty graphic."

Avery folded her arms. "Go ahead. I'll be fine."

Dr. Riggins glanced at Jaxon for confirmation, and Jaxon gestured for him to continue.

He indicated a whiteboard on the wall, then flipped it over on the stand to reveal numerous photographs of Wade Mulligan's body in various states—clothed, bloody and dead, on the floor of the bedroom where he'd been murdered, and others of him naked on the autopsy table.

Jaxon pointed to the pictures. "There are the photographs the ME took of Mulligan when he got him on the table."

Jaxon noted the gashes on the man's chest, and glanced at Avery to see if she was okay. Her face had paled slightly, her lips pinched.

Dr. Riggins pointed to several of the stab wounds. "If you look at the angle of these, they all slant the same direction, indicating that they were done by a right-handed person."

Which made sense. Hank was right-handed. He pointed to the numerous small stab wounds. "Those were the wounds Hank inflicted."

"But look here." Dr. Riggins used a pointer to highlight another stab wound, this one slightly different. "It's not only deeper and wider but slants the opposite direction."

Jaxon's heart hammered. "That one was made by someone other than Hank. By someone left-handed."

Dr. Riggins pushed his glasses up his nose with a smile. "Exactly."

Avery made a low sound in her throat. "What are you saying?"

Adrenaline rushed through Jaxon. This was what they needed, some concrete evidence to support the theory that there had been another perpetrator.

"It means that a second person stabbed Wade," Jaxon said.

"Not only that," Dr. Riggins said as he pointed to the wound again, "but this wound was the fatal one. It sliced through the aorta. Mulligan probably died within seconds."

Jaxon gritted his teeth. This should be good news.

Except that Avery was left-handed.

AVERY MENTALLY DIGESTED the implications of the ME's report. "That means Hank was telling the truth."

"It could mean a second person actually killed Mulligan," Jaxon said quietly.

Avery glanced at her hands, her eyes widening. "My God, I'm left-handed."

She staggered back against the table. "Hank thought I stabbed Wade. And I…don't remember what happened that night." Fear clogged her throat. "What if I did do it?"

Regret flashed in Jaxon's eyes. "Avery, don't jump to conclusions. You were just a child."

Avery rubbed the scar on her wrist. "I didn't want to remember." Her breath caught. "But then I thought Hank was guilty. I didn't see any reason to relive it." Maybe she should try harder now.

If she could recall the details of that night, if she'd witnessed the murder, she might be able to identify the killer.

"Ms. Tierney," Dr. Riggins said. "The wound made by the left hand was the fatal one and much deeper than the other wounds, which appear more superficial. It tore through muscle and tissue. But I doubt a nine-year-old girl would have that kind of strength."

Relief filled Avery. "If you show this to a judge, he'll have to stop the execution and grant a new investigation."

Jaxon scrubbed a hand over the back of his neck. "I wish it was that simple. But the prosecutor can easily argue that Hank used his left hand at some point. Maybe he grabbed the knife with his left hand at first because he was holding Mulligan down with his right, or he dropped it at some point and then retrieved it with his other hand."

Avery's hopes wilted.

"Don't get too discouraged, Avery," Jaxon said. "This is a start. But we need more." He turned back to the forensic specialist. "Is there anything else you can tell us from the body?"

Dr. Riggins studied the photographs intently. He pointed to a cut on the man's right wrist. "The only defensive wound Mulligan sustained is that cut. Which suggests that he raised his arm in an attempt to deflect the blow from the left-handed attacker."

"So that wound, which was the killing blow, was delivered first," Jaxon said.

Avery's hope stirred to life again. "That confirms Hank's story, that Mulligan was dead when he stabbed him."

Dr. Riggins pulled a hand down his chin. "Based on angle and depth of the wounds, I would testify that there were two different attackers."

"But we still need proof that someone else was there," Jaxon pointed out.

Avery's head began to pound. "Maybe it's time I work

on recovering my memory. If I saw the killer and can identify him, or her, then I can free my brother."

JAXON FELT THE fear emanating from Avery as he drove her back to her house.

She'd blocked out the traumatic events of that night because they were so horrible. Reliving them would be a nightmare come true.

But would it help her heal?

And how could she go on if she continued to be plagued with guilt over Hank's incarceration? Worse, how would she live with herself if she learned she had killed Mulligan?

He pulled down the road leading to Avery's but slowed as he approached, a bad feeling in his gut.

Avery suddenly sat up straighter and gasped as they parked.

Jaxon's pulse hammered when he saw the words painted on the front door.

"An eye for an eye. Hank Tierney should die."

Chapter Thirteen

Avery stumbled from the SUV, shock rolling through her. "Who did this?"

She turned to Jaxon, hands on her hips. "Who cares enough about Hank and a murder he supposedly committed twenty years ago to torment me?"

"The person who really killed Mulligan," Jaxon said matter-of-factly.

Fear shot through Avery, and she pivoted to search the street, then the woods behind her house.

Jaxon also visually searched the perimeter as they approached the front door. "There's another possibility. There are always lunatics who follow death row cases. One of them could have paid you a visit because he knows you're trying to stop the execution. You'd be surprised at the fanatics who protest against the death penalty while others lobby for it. Some of them even write prisoners and offer conjugal visits and marriage proposals."

"But the warden said that Hank hadn't had any visitors, not until I asked to see him."

Jaxon snapped his fingers as if a thought just occurred to him. "I'll call the warden and ask if Hank received any suspicious mail. It's possible the killer wrote him."

Avery started to touch the wording on the door, but Jaxon caught her hand. "Don't. I want a crime team to process this place. Maybe whoever left that message also left a fingerprint."

He stepped aside to call the crime team.

Although her first instinct was to run inside, grab cleaning supplies and erase the ugly message, Avery stepped back from the door, knowing Jaxon was right.

Memories of her teenage years bombarded her. The other teens teasing her, calling her a murderer's daughter. A murderer's sister.

Making jokes about when she would go ballistic and start her own killing spree.

One day a group had painted the word *killer* all over her locker.

After that, others had taunted her with the name. They said she had bad blood. That she'd end up in jail just like her father and brother.

Once she'd even considered getting a gun and firing it at the next person who tortured her with ugly words.

She'd even sneaked out of the group home that night and met a guy on the streets in a dark alley, one who'd promised her a Saturday-night special.

But she'd seen another little girl that night. A tiny little thing walking with her mother. They were holding hands singing some silly song about a frog. They'd looked so normal.

Her heart had ached. She'd never had normal.

Heaven help her, but she'd wanted normal. Wanted a family and someone to love her.

A light had flickered in her head—if she shot someone, she'd never have that life. She'd become exactly what the others kids called her. A killer. She'd prove that she had bad blood. And she'd end up in prison like her father and brother.

So she'd turned around and walked down the street, following the woman and child. She'd stood in the shadows and watched them enter the Humane Society. A few minutes later, they came out with a scruffy-looking dog.

The little girl and mother had laughed and giggled as the puppy licked the child's face and nuzzled up to her.

After they left, Avery had walked into the Humane Society and strolled through, looking at the lost and abandoned animals. She knew just how they felt and wanted to take them all home that day.

But the group home didn't allow pets, so she'd offered to volunteer at the adoption center.

"Avery, are you all right?"

She looked up at him as he pocketed the phone. So much had happened in the two days since she'd met him.

Hank could still die.

A strangled sob escaped her, and she spun around to avoid letting him see her cry.

"What if I did do it?"

"Aw, Avery, I don't think you did."

Then he slid his arms around her from behind. Unable to help herself, she leaned into him, turned around and buried herself in his arms.

JAXON STROKED AVERY's back, her warm body heating his own. He only meant to comfort her, but her fingers trailed across his chest, and his lungs squeezed for air.

She felt so sweet and hot at the same time, and the feeling stirred protective instincts that made him want to alleviate all the pain in her life. She also aroused a passionate need inside him that made him want to carry her to bed and make love to her until dawn.

Make love?

Hell. What was wrong with him? Avery was a…a woman who'd been victimized. Who needed his professional help.

She lifted her head and looked up at him with those

sensual, lonely eyes, and his heart tripped, robbing all rational thoughts from his head.

He pressed a hand to her cheek, ordering himself to pull away. They were in the middle of a crime scene.

But her eyes fluttered, and she emitted a soft purr that ripped away his resolve, and he lowered his head. He hesitated, his lips an inch from her mouth, and searched her face.

The flare of need in her expression triggered his own, and he was lost.

He closed his lips over hers, his heart hammering wildly as she kissed him in return. She threaded her hands in his hair, digging her fingers deeper as she pulled him closer.

He forced himself to be gentle when he wanted to swing her up, take her inside and prove to her that men could be gentle and loving at the same time.

Heat exploded between them, her breath rasping against his neck as he ended the kiss. But she cradled his face between her hands and looked at him again. Heat flared as she traced one finger over his mouth.

He sucked in a breath, allowing her to take her time, to memorize his lips the way he wanted to memorize every inch of her.

But his cell phone buzzed on his hip, and he stilled. What the hell was he doing?

He eased away from her, aware that their breathing sounded raspy in the silence.

"Avery?"

Her eyes were swimming with desire and other emotions he didn't understand.

"I shouldn't have done that."

A small smile tugged at her lips. "I wanted it."

That admission made him want to kiss her again. But his phone buzzed once more, and the sound of an engine broke the spell.

He stepped back and answered his phone as he went to meet the crime team. Damn, it was his director on the phone.

"Ward, I need an update," the director said in a demanding tone.

Jaxon grimaced. The last thing his boss wanted was to know that he'd kissed Avery Tierney. And that he believed Hank was innocent. "I've been talking to people involved in the original investigation to verify stories."

"What the hell does that mean?"

That I think you made a mistake. But he needed concrete proof before he confronted him.

He lowered his voice so Avery wouldn't hear. "You wanted me to make sure the conviction wasn't overturned, so I'm reviewing the case. If it's solid, there's nothing to worry about." There, that was a roundabout answer.

The director heaved a breath. "All right. Just talk to D.A. William Snyderman. He was the assistant D.A. back then. He'll confirm that we ran the investigation by the book."

He was also friends with the director. Now Jaxon understood even more his boss's determination to keep the execution on track. Both his and the D.A.'s reputations depended on it.

"I plan to," Jaxon said. "But I have to go now."

Three crime team workers exited the van, and he pocketed his phone and introduced himself. Avery was standing by his SUV, her arms wrapped around her waist as she stared at the ugly taunt on her door.

Lieutenant Carl Dothan introduced him to the other two crime investigators—Samantha Franks and Wynn Pollock. "What happened?" Dothan asked.

Jaxon explained about Avery's connection to Hank Tierney. "Someone vandalized the outside of the house and painted that threat on Ms. Tierney's door."

"How's the inside of the house?" Franks asked.

Self-disgust ripped through Jaxon. He hadn't even checked. He'd been too busy kissing Avery.

"I haven't been inside, didn't want to contaminate anything out here." Sounded feasible. "I called you to start processing the outside and canvass the neighbors to see if they witnessed anything." He gestured toward the house. "I'll search the inside now."

"You didn't think whoever did this might still be around?" Dothan asked.

Jaxon's gut tightened. "There was no sign of that, no car or anyone on foot when we arrived. Ms. Tierney was understandably upset, so I called you. She received a disturbing phone call earlier and is pretty shaken up."

Lieutenant Dothan gave a clipped nod, then turned to Franks and Pollock. "Franks, canvass the neighborhood. Pollock, start with the photographs, and I'll search the yard and drive for forensics."

They dispersed, and Jaxon walked back to Avery. "Stay here. I'm going to search the inside of the house and see if whoever did this broke in."

Something he should have done already. But he'd been too distracted by Avery.

Dammit, if he messed up, it might mean the difference between making a valid case to save Hank and not.

He couldn't let himself be sidetracked again.

"Stay here," Jaxon told Avery.

She shook her head. "Let me go with you. I'll be able to tell if anything is missing or if someone's been inside."

His gaze locked with hers for a tense second. Other emotions flickered there as well—regret that he'd kissed her?

She didn't regret it, though.

Avery had never been kissed. Not by a man.

She thought she never would be, that she wouldn't be able to be intimate.

But she felt safe in Jaxon's arms. Safe in his kiss.

She wanted more.

Emotions mingled with desire, stirring relief and need at the same time. Maybe she could be normal after all.

Maybe she could even have a relationship and a family of her own someday.

"Stay behind me," Jaxon ordered. "Is there a back door we can go in while CSI processes the front door?"

She nodded, trembling slightly as they walked to the back entrance of the house. She scanned the backyard and woods beyond, but everything seemed quiet. Still. The wind had even died down, yet the darkness hovering over the yard gave her an eerie feeling.

She climbed the two steps to the screened back porch, peering inside at the rustic table and chairs. Nothing looked out of place or as if anyone had been inside.

"Let me," Jaxon said when she reached for the doorknob.

She stepped aside, her body tingling as his hard chest brushed hers. He jiggled the door, and it screeched open. Jaxon arched a brow at her, and she tensed.

"It was locked."

He gestured for her to stay behind him, then inched inside. The back door stood ajar, causing fear to course up her spine.

Jaxon pulled his gun and held it at the ready, then tiptoed toward the door. He eased inside, looking left and right. Avery peered over his shoulder, staying close to him as they entered.

The kitchen looked untouched, as did the den and connected dining area.

Jaxon swung his gun toward the stairs. "Upstairs?" he said in a low voice.

"Two bedrooms. First one is mine, second is a guest room."

Jaxon slowly inched his way up, Avery on his heels. He

paused on every other step to listen for sounds of an intruder, but the only sound Avery heard was their breathing and the slow hum of the heater.

The curtains fluttered in her room, jerking her attention to her bed.

Nausea gripped her stomach as she realized someone had been inside.

Pictures of Wade Mulligan's mutilated dead body were scattered across her bed.

But the picture in the middle was the one that made her cringe.

It was a photograph of her with a knife stuck in the middle.

JAXON RELEASED A string of expletives. Dammit, Avery didn't deserve this.

He glanced over his shoulder at her and saw her sway slightly. Worried, he slid an arm around her waist. "I'm here, Avery. It's going to be all right."

"Surely one of the neighbors saw something."

"Hopefully so." He took her hand and guided her back to the stairs. "Don't touch anything. Maybe this creep left a print and we can nail him."

AVERY TIERNEY HAD found her presents. The fear on her face had been priceless and meant that scare tactics might work on her.

Although that Texas Ranger was a problem.

But processing the scene would take time.

Time away from looking into Hank Tierney's case.

Time was all that was necessary. If the Ranger and Avery didn't find the truth, Hank Tierney would die.

Then there would be no reason to reopen the case, and Avery and the Ranger would have to stop asking questions.

Chapter Fourteen

Jaxon ushered Avery outside and encouraged her to sit in the SUV and wait. He strode over to Lieutenant Dothan and explained that they needed to process the interior of the house.

"I'll do it myself," Dothan said.

"Thanks. I'm going to take Avery somewhere safe for the night. Let me know what you find."

Dothan agreed, and Jaxon joined Avery. When he cranked the engine, Avery frowned. "Where are we going?"

He had to get her away from her house. Knowing her room had been violated had to be unsettling for her, especially that damn picture of her with the knife in it. That was a blatant threat. "To my place. The crime team will call me with their findings."

"Your place?" Avery asked in a soft rasp.

Damn. The earlier kiss taunted him. He hadn't thought how his suggestion might sound. "I just want you to be safe tonight." He forced his eyes on the road. "Don't worry, Avery. You'll have your own room."

"I wasn't worried," she said softly.

His gaze cut to hers. The husky sound in her voice matched the simmering desire in those eyes.

Dammit, he was in trouble.

Heat speared him, but he forced his attention back to the road. He'd already screwed up by kissing her earlier instead of searching the house before he called CSI. Hell, what if the intruder had been there when they arrived?

He could have caught him in the act.

Although it was doubtful that he'd been present. Not that he couldn't have sneaked out the back and disappeared into the woods....

"Uh, Jaxon," Avery said as they drove into town. "I don't have clothes or a toothbrush with me."

He hadn't considered that. "Not a problem. I'll stop and let you pick up whatever you need."

He veered into the parking lot of the discount store and parked. "I'll call the prison warden and ask him to collect Hank's mail while you run inside."

"Can I see Hank again?" Avery asked.

"I'll ask."

She thanked him, then jumped out and hurried into the store.

Jaxon punched the number for the warden, keeping an eye on the door of the store in case someone had followed Avery.

"We typically examine the mail when it's delivered, although sometimes that takes time and we fall behind," the warden said. "I don't recall anything suspicious. Just the typical hate mail along with the sympathizers for his cause. A couple of offers for conjugal visits. Another group wanting to rally to save him."

"Just box it all up. I need to study the correspondence."

The warden agreed, and Jaxon hung up. If Mulligan's killer hadn't trashed Avery's house, then someone else had.

Maybe he'd find a clue as to his or her identity in those letters.

Or...it was possible that the killer felt remorse over Hank's upcoming execution.

Enough so that he or she might have contacted Hank?

AVERY STRUGGLED TO shake off her nerves as she stepped on the front porch of Jaxon's ranch house. The sprawling land with horses roaming free and cattle grazing was a picture of beauty. It reminded her of old Western movies about families working together and riding and…loving each other.

Like a real family.

"This is beautiful," Avery said. "You live here alone?"

Jaxon nodded. "Yeah, I bought it a while back. I need to hire some help, though. With me gone working cases, I can't manage it by myself."

Nerves fluttered in her stomach. Being in his home felt… intimate.

But he'd only brought her here because she'd been threatened.

He probably brought women here all the time. Maybe not from his cases, but a man like Jaxon probably had a half dozen lovers waiting for him to call. She was probably interfering with a hot, sexy night with one of them this evening.

He opened the door and ushered her inside. "Make yourself at home, Avery. It's not fancy, but it's comfortable."

Avery admired the rustic pine floors, the masculine furniture and the fireplace. It looked perfect. Like a home where a man lived.

A painting of several wild mustangs graced the wall above the couch, while another one of the famous Cherokee Crossing where the Native Americans and settlers had met to build a town hall together hung above an oak table.

"I don't have much food in the house," he admitted in a voice laced with regret. "But I can fix us omelets."

"That's fine," Avery said, a tingle spreading up her back at the idea of Jaxon cooking for her.

He's just doing his job, she reminded herself.

Except that kiss had been sensual. Not just Jaxon doing his job. At least she didn't think it was.

It felt more like Jaxon being the sexy protector. As if for a moment, Jaxon had wanted her.

But he'd pulled back and hadn't pushed her. Which made her respect him even more. Some men would have taken advantage.

But not Jaxon.

"There's a hall bathroom here," he said. Then he showed her to the bedroom. "This is my room, but you can sleep in here tonight. There's a full bath that joins the room if you want to wash up while I throw together some food."

She glanced at the log-cabin quilt on the sleigh bed and once again felt as if she'd come home. "Thanks, I think I will." Just seeing those ugly pictures made her feel dirty all over.

He returned to the living room, grabbed the bag of items she'd bought at the discount store and set them in the room. She grabbed the bag and ducked into the bathroom.

One glance in the mirror and she grimaced. Her hair was a wreck, what little makeup she'd put on this morning was long gone and her eyes looked…frightened.

Was she frightened of Jaxon? Or simply scared of the way he made her feel?

She flipped on the shower water and cranked it up, then peeled off her clothes. Her nipples budded to stiff peaks, her body trembling as she remembered Jaxon's lips on hers. God help her, but she wanted to feel them on her mouth again.

She closed her eyes as the hot water sluiced over her, and she imagined the door sliding open and Jaxon stepping inside with her. She could almost feel his big hands running over her shoulders, down her arms, then touching her waist as he drew her closer. She leaned her head back, her body tingling as she imagined his lips on her neck, his tongue teasing her earlobe.

Naked body against naked body…

She jerked her eyes open, so hot she could hardly breathe.

What in the world was happening to her? She never fantasized about being with a man....

Disturbed by her train of thought, especially in light of the fact that she needed Jaxon to help clear Hank, she flipped the water to cold, rinsed off, then climbed out and dried off. She slipped on the pajamas she'd bought to sleep in, then brushed through her damp hair.

Jaxon was not interested in her. He had simply been comforting her because she'd been a trembling mess earlier. He would have done the same for any woman who'd been in need.

She was just so inexperienced that she'd read more into it.

She absolutely had to get control of herself and focus on finding Hank's killer.

For heaven's sake, he could be put to death by the end of the week.

And that would be her fault.

Reality sobered her, and she opened the door. Steam oozed from the bathroom, and her breath caught at the sight of Jaxon by the bed.

"I put clean sheets on for you," he said.

Her gaze met his, her earlier fantasy taunting her. She wanted to ask him to join her in bed, to beg him to touch her all over and kiss her again.

His gaze raked over her, heat simmering between them.

Instead of coming toward her, though, he backed toward the kitchen. "The food is ready."

Disappointment snaked through her. But freeing Hank was more important than her own needs, so she followed him into the kitchen.

JAXON CLEANED UP the dishes after their meal and was grateful when Avery retired to the bedroom. Having her in his kitchen, in his house, his shower and now his bedroom was wreaking havoc on his common sense.

It also felt intimate, something he hadn't shared with a woman in… Something he'd never shared with a woman. He liked his bachelor status, his nights of sex, but his mornings without a woman to push him for more.

Oddly the thought of waking up beside Avery didn't panic him.

It should, dammit.

He knew he wouldn't sleep much tonight, not with Avery in his bed. Not unless he joined her, and that wasn't going to happen.

Determined to focus on work, he spread out the files on the Tierney case and studied them once more. He scribbled Mulligan's name at the top of a legal pad, then Hank and Avery's names below.

As much as he hated to admit it, Avery was still a suspect. She was left-handed, and even though she had only been nine, fear could trigger an adrenaline rush that could have given her the strength to stab Mulligan.

If she had killed him, it would also explain why she'd blocked out the traumatic memory. And an attorney could plead self-defense.

But how would Avery handle knowing that she was the reason her brother had been behind bars for twenty years?

She already harbored too much guilt.

He rubbed a hand over his chin. Hell, did he honestly believe Avery had killed her foster father?

He scribbled the names of the D.A. and public defender who'd handled the case, knowing he needed to talk to them.

Next he listed the social workers—Delia Hanover and Erma Brant.

Delia had claimed not to know about the abuse. What about Erma?

He would speak to her next.

Below those names he wrote a list of the foster children they knew about.

Shane Fowler—body shop owner—claimed to know of the abuse.

Lois Thacker—now a cop—knew of abuse. Had the right temperament? But right-handed.

Lenny Ames—committed suicide.

Dotty—dead.

Imogene Wilson—in a psychiatric hospital—confessed to murder, but delusional.

Imogene's brother, BJ—drug addict who hated Mulligan—no solid alibi.

Any one of the fosters had motive.

He remembered the autopsy and realized he needed to find out which one of them had been left-handed.

Other than Avery.

AVERY CURLED INTO Jaxon's bed, the day's events traipsing through her mind. She and Jaxon had made headway toward proving Hank's innocence. At least the autopsy might help.

But time was running out.

She tossed and turned, but finally buried her head into the pillow. Although Jaxon had changed the bedding, his strong masculine scent permeated the room. She closed her eyes and imagined his big muscular arms enveloping her, and her breathing steadied.

Jaxon was in the next room. He would protect her.

She was safe for tonight.

Tomorrow they would find a way to clear her brother.

Slowly she drifted to sleep, but the nightmare came again....

She was back at the Mulligans' old house, curled in her bed, the covers tugged up to her neck. Joleen was gone, and Wade had come in, blustering again.

He didn't like the dinner she'd cooked for him and Hank. She'd made tomato soup and grilled-cheese sandwiches, and he wanted meat.

She clenched her teddy bear, checked to make sure the stick was still under the bed, closed her eyes and finally fell asleep, praying he'd leave her alone tonight. But some time later, the door burst open, jarring her. Then Hank's voice.

"Leave her alone," Hank shouted.

The fists came next. Hank was fighting Wade, but Wade was dragging him across the hall back to his room.

Rain pattered on the tin roof. Suddenly the wind swirled through the house. She looked over and saw the curtains flapping against the windowsill.

Then a voice whispered, "It'll be all right."

A woman's voice... But whose?

Footsteps sounded and fear clawed at her chest. He was coming into her bedroom again.

She screamed, and then everything went dark....

Some time later, Hank's shout jolted her from the darkness. He was beside the bed, pulling something from her hands. She clenched it tighter, but he pried her fingers loose.

"Give it to me, sis," he said in a low voice. "It's okay now."

Her fingers loosened. The room swirled, colors dancing in front of her eyes. Red, then black. Blood. Everywhere.

She looked down and saw blood on her hands.

Then Hank knelt over Wade. Wade was on the floor, not moving. More blood. Hank raised the knife and jabbed it into the man's chest.

She screamed again, a scream that echoed off the cold walls....

"Avery!" The door burst open, and she jerked awake. Her heart was racing, her body trembling. For a moment, she was so lost in the nightmare that she was disoriented. She didn't know where she was.

Didn't realize who the man was in the doorway.

Mulligan... He'd come back to get her.

She cried out as he strode to the bed. The mattress sagged; then he reached for her, and she swung her fists at him.

She had to get away….

JAXON BRACED HIMSELF as he drew Avery against him, but she beat at him with her fists, her scream punctuating the air as she tried to push him away.

Dammit, she was in the throes of a nightmare.

Or…a memory.

He murmured soft words, trying to soothe her. "Avery, wake up, it's me, Jaxon."

Sweat rolled down his neck. Her scream had sent a streak of cold terror through him. He'd run to the bedroom in a panic, fearing the worst. Someone was trying to kill her. Someone who'd followed them here and broken in.

Her cries echoed in the room, a haunting sound that made his blood go cold.

He cradled her closer. Avery was safe. At least physically.

"It's over, I've got you," he whispered. "You're safe, Avery. He can't hurt you anymore."

Except that dead man was still hurting her because he couldn't tell them who'd killed him.

Avery stilled, her breath rasping out as she opened her eyes. She blinked several times, obviously trying to focus.

"It's me—Jaxon," he said huskily. "I'm here, Avery."

She clutched his chest, her eyes pained as she looked into his eyes. "There was someone else there that night," she said in a raspy voice.

"What?"

"I remembered," she said. "The window, it was open. I felt the wind blowing in, saw the curtains flapping."

Jaxon's pulse kicked up. "You saw someone?"

She pushed a tangled strand of hair from her damp cheek. "No, but I heard a voice. She told me it was going to be okay."

"She?"

Avery nodded. "Yes, it was a woman's voice. She… comforted me. Then…everything went black."

"Did you recognize the voice. Was it Joleen? Maybe Imogene?"

Confusion clouded her face again, and another sob tore from her throat. "I don't know. It was just a whisper."

Pain wrenched Avery's eyes, and she released him and stared at her hands. "But…when the darkness lifted, I looked down. Hank was there, telling me it would be all right. He was taking something from my hands."

She trembled more violently. "I had the knife in my hands, the bloody knife." Her tormented gaze met his. "God, Jaxon…I think I might have killed Wade."

Chapter Fifteen

Jaxon stroked Avery's back, hating the fear in her voice.

"What if I did it?" Tears streaked from her big eyes. "Maybe Hank was right. I stabbed him, and then Hank took the knife from me and cleaned it off so no one would know." Her voice cracked. "He stabbed Wade to cover up for me, and I let him."

Jaxon's chest tightened. That version fit—the reason police had found no other prints than Hank's was that he'd wiped them off to erase Avery's.

"I have to come forward, to confess," she said, her voice panicked.

Jaxon gripped her arms and forced her to look at him. "Stop it, Avery. If it had happened like that, you were only a child and blocked out the memory to protect your mind until you were ready to deal with it."

"Well, I'm not a child anymore. I can free Hank."

Jaxon shook his head. "It wouldn't work. At this point, no one would believe you. They'd think you were just making it up to save Hank."

"But if Hank and I both tell the same story—"

"Do you really think your brother will agree to that?"

She wiped at her eyes. "I'll convince him to."

"I'm sorry, Avery. No judge would buy it." He hesitated. "Besides, I don't believe that you killed Mulligan."

"Why not?" Avery cried. "He was attacking me. I could have brought a kitchen knife to bed with me earlier."

"Did you?" he asked.

She looked down at his hands where they held her, confusion marring her face. "I...I'm not sure. But I could have. I was afraid. I knew he'd come in because Joleen was gone for the night."

Jaxon gently tilted her chin up. "Avery, do you remember taking a knife from the kitchen?"

Her face crumpled, and she shook her head. "No, but that doesn't mean I didn't do it."

He stroked her hair back from her cheek. "You said something about the window being open. Did you leave it open at night?"

She jerked her gaze toward him, seemingly surprised by the question. "No. I always wanted it closed. I was scared a monster might get in."

Of course, there was one already in the house.

"And you said you heard a woman's voice?"

"Yes. She whispered that it would be all right."

"Was the voice Joleen's?"

"I don't know. It was really low and I didn't see her face."

AVERY HAD DOUBTED everything about that horrible night. But she hadn't imagined that woman's voice.

Someone else had been in the house that night.

That woman could have killed Wade.

"What do you think she meant? That everything would be all right? Were you crying? Was Wade in the room at the time?"

Avery closed her eyes, desperate to sort through the memory. "I don't remember. Just that I was hiding under the covers, and she touched my arm and squeezed it, then whispered to me."

"Did you hear any other noise? Did Wade come in the room when she was there, or was he already dead?"

Her head throbbed from trying to recall the details. "I... don't know. Everything is so jumbled. I...I remember hearing footsteps, and then...I felt the cold air from the window."

"What did you do then?"

Avery massaged the scar on her wrist. "I was hiding in the bed, and I waited until it was quiet. Then I looked down and saw the knife. It was all bloody...."

"What happened next?"

"I...think I blacked out for another minute. The next thing I remember is Hank taking the knife from me. Then he was standing over Wade's body. He raised the knife and drove it down into him. Then I screamed. And he...he stabbed him over and over again."

Jaxon rubbed her arms. "Who called the police? Did you phone them?"

She blinked hard, a headache pulsing behind her eyes. Finally she shook her head. "No. I...just remember crying and seeing Hank with that knife. Then suddenly the police burst in and everyone was yelling. Then some female officer wrapped me in a blanket, and I saw lights from the police car swirling in the dark and an ambulance, and a big policeman dragged Hank toward his car."

Her body shook with emotions as another flood of tears rained down her face. They had ripped Hank from her life that day, and she'd thought she lost him forever.

And she *would* lose him if she didn't find a way to stop the execution.

So who was the woman she'd heard whispering to her that night?

LATER AT THE PRISON, Jaxon explained to the warden his reasons for requesting Hank's mail. "Someone has been threatening Ms. Tierney. There might be a clue as to who it is in the correspondence. Can you think of anyone specific that's written to him? Someone suspicious?"

"To tell you the truth," the warden said, "we haven't had time to sort through it all. The past six months, after that reporter wrote the story on death row and mentioned Tierney, we've been flooded with mail. So have the prisoners awaiting execution."

"Let me have the mail. I'll look through it, then have the FBI lab analyze it. We have specialists who can detect patterns, threats, look at handwriting analysis, even search for underlying meanings in messages."

"Fine, take them. We've got our hands full here."

Avery cleared her throat. "I want to see my brother again."

The warden graced her with a sympathetic look. "Of course."

He led them into the hallway and arranged for them to visit in a private room as he'd done before. "Have you found any evidence to exonerate Hank?"

Jaxon clenched his jaw. "We're still working on it."

Avery had lapsed into a worried silence, and remained quiet as the guard escorted them to a visitors' room.

Hands clenched, Avery slid into the chair in front of the table, but her gaze was glued to her scar. She was obviously pushing herself to recall the details of that night.

The door squeaked open, and Hank shuffled in, chained and handcuffed again. Avery looked up at him with such a deep sadness that a knot formed inside Jaxon's belly.

Would she survive if they didn't save her brother?

AVERY SWALLOWED HARD to keep from bursting into tears. Hank's face looked bruised and battered, his arms scraped, and he was limping as if he was in pain.

Even worse, despair darkened his eyes.

Metal clanged as he dropped into the chair. "You came back? Why?"

Avery flinched at the distrust in his voice. But she deserved it. "I told you I was going to get you free, and we're working on it." She gestured toward Jaxon. "We've been questioning everyone we can think of who might know what happened that night."

A faint spark of hope flickered in his eyes for a second, then disappeared. "But you still don't know who killed Mulligan."

Avery laid her hand over his. He stiffened, and looked at her hand as if it felt foreign to be touched.

At least gently. He'd been beaten on for years. That was obvious.

"No," Jaxon said. "But we questioned some of the other foster children placed with the Mulligans, and they confirmed Mulligan's abusive behavior. Their testimony will work in your favor."

A muscle twitched in Hank's forehead. "But it won't get me off?"

Avery had to offer him some hope. "It proves others had motive, so we can argue reasonable doubt."

Hank balled his hands into fists, but Avery didn't let go of his hand.

"But none of those other fosters were at the house," Hank said, his voice deflated.

Avery took a deep breath. "I think someone was," she said. "I remembered something, Hank. I woke up and the window was open in my room."

Hank narrowed his eyes. "So?"

"I always kept it shut, remember? I was scared of the monsters in the woods."

"The only monster was Mulligan," Hank muttered.

She rubbed her finger over his knuckle. "True. But I remembered something else. I heard a woman's voice."

Hank went very still. "A woman? Who?"

"I don't know yet." Avery's lungs strained for air as panic threatened. "But I distinctly remember hearing her voice. I was hiding under the covers, and she touched my arm and murmured that everything was going to be all right."

Hank stared at their hands again, emotions rippling across his face. "How does that help us?"

Jaxon's dark eyes promised nothing, making Avery want to cry again. "If Avery remembers that a woman was there, we'll find her. She could have come in and killed Mulligan. Avery was in shock from witnessing the murder and picked up the knife. Then you thought she'd killed him, so you wiped off the prints in an attempt to cover for her."

"You didn't see her because she climbed out my window," Avery said. "I remember it being open and the wind blowing."

Hank dropped his head forward, his voice a self-deprecating murmur. "So I wiped off the only evidence that could potentially clear me."

Pain wrapped itself around Avery and wouldn't let go. Hank was right.

Between the two of them, they had let the real killer go free.

JAXON STUDIED HANK. He had been hardened by prison. Hell, he'd been hardened by life long before he was locked in a cell.

He'd been abused and was filled with rage that night, but maybe he remembered more than he'd revealed. Some detail that could help Jaxon crack the case.

"Hank, what about you? What do you recall from that night?"

Hank's eyes flared with suspicion. "You think I did it?"

"No," Jaxon said, realizing how much he meant it. "And I'm trying to help you and your sister." In spite of the fact that his boss would be more than pissed. "So cut the bull and tell us everything that happened that night."

"I already have." Hank's voice sounded raw with worry. "When the old lady left, I knew Mulligan would go in Avery's room that night, so I took a knife from the kitchen and hid it in the bed. Later, when I heard him going toward her room, I tried to stop him. But he hit me and tied me to the bed." He paused, his breath raspy. "A few minutes later, I heard Avery screaming and I was furious. I twisted and turned until I got hold of the knife and cut myself free." He ran a hand over his shaved head. "When I went in and saw Avery with that bloody knife in her hands and Mulligan lying there dead, I freaked out. I figured she'd killed him, so I took the knife from her and wiped it clean and then I stabbed him."

Jaxon's pulse clamored. "You said you had a knife in your bedroom. But Avery had another knife and you took it and used it to stab Mulligan." He paused. "What happened to the first knife?"

Hank pinched the bridge of his nose. "I don't know. I think I had it when I went in the room, but maybe I dropped it somewhere."

A tense silence stretched for a full minute. "I'm going to ask the D.A. and your defense attorney," Jaxon said. "It should have shown up in the crime scene photos."

Hank made a low sound in his throat. "Even if you find the other knife, won't the lawyers argue that Avery had it with her?"

"That's possible," Jaxon said. "But I don't like the fact that there was no mention of it at the trial. That makes me wonder why."

Avery squeezed her brother's hand. "Hang in there, Hank."

His defeated look tore at Jaxon. Hank Tierney didn't expect anyone to believe him or help him.

"One more question," Jaxon said. "Hank, do you know who called the police? Was it you or Avery?"

Hank shook his head, his eyes flat again. "No. I didn't call them. And Avery was too upset. She couldn't stop crying."

Jaxon swallowed a curse. That was another question for the D.A. and defense attorney. Had a neighbor phoned it in? And how did the neighbor know unless he or she had seen something? The houses were too far apart for one of them to have heard Avery crying.

Unless the caller had been inside the house....

Which meant the killer might have called 911 after he or she left.

LEAVING HANK IN prison ripped at Avery's nerves.

She and Jaxon had to find this mystery woman.

He drove to a set of office buildings not too far from the prison. "Wright Pullman was your brother's defense attorney," he said to Avery. "Do you remember him?"

Avery searched her memory banks. An image of a young man in a suit at the courthouse with Hank flashed back. "Vaguely."

"Did he question you?" Jaxon asked as they walked up to Pullman's office door.

"I honestly don't remember," Avery said. "I was pretty out of it back then. I just remember begging them not to take Hank away."

Hank had been her only safety net.

Jaxon spoke to a receptionist, who asked them to wait in the front room. Avery noted the office furniture was cheap, the paintings generic, the carpet low-grade.

"I did a little research on Pullman," Jaxon said when the receptionist disappeared into the back. "He's nothing more than a glorified ambulance chaser."

The receptionist returned. "Mr. Pullman will see you now."

Avery followed Jaxon into the man's office, her gaze surveying Wright Pullman. He was older now, in his forties probably, with a bad comb-over, wire-rimmed glasses and a beard. His suit looked as cheap as his office furniture.

Jaxon quickly made introductions and explained the reason for their visit.

Pullman toyed with a pen on his desk. "I figured someone would show up asking questions. Always happens with a death row case."

"Do you remember my brother?" Avery asked.

"Hard to forget." The lawyer's chair squeaked as he shifted. "He was one of my first cases. I was just a public defender back then, swamped with cases that nobody wanted." He crossed his legs. "But that one stuck out in my mind."

"Why is that?" Jaxon asked.

"'Cause the kid was only fourteen. But it was obvious he was guilty. He admitted to stabbing Mulligan a dozen times." He shot Avery a look of regret. "I know you're probably grasping for some way to save him now, but no one coerced that confession from him. And he was dangerous. Hell, he scared me. I've never seen a kid with so much rage."

Avery planted her hands on his desk and leaned forward. "Yes, he was full of rage because Wade Mulligan was molesting me. Did you know that when you went to court?"

The man's freckled skin paled. "Look, I did everything I could. I tried to cut a deal with the assistant D.A. who prosecuted the case, but he refused. He was a cocky bastard who wanted to make a name for himself, and that case got a lot of press."

Avery shivered at the memory of reporters dogging her.

"The A.D.A. used the shock factor of those photos of the multiple stab wounds to convince the jury that Tierney killed Mulligan in cold blood, and that he was a danger to society."

"How about arguing that there were extenuating circumstances?" Jaxon asked. "That Hank was defending himself and his sister from abuse?"

"I…didn't know," Pullman said in a low voice.

"Because you didn't do your job," Jaxon snapped. "You readily accepted the kid's confession at face value. If you'd talked to the social workers and other foster kids placed with the Mulligans as I have, you would have realized that Hank was protecting Avery that night."

Pullman's thin lips darted into a frown. "Listen here, I did do my job. But I was young, overworked, and the A.D.A. was determined to make an example out of Tierney."

"Do you remember photographs of the crime scene?" Jaxon asked.

Pullman's eyes narrowed. "What are you getting at?"

"Hank Tierney claims he had a knife in his room with him. That Mulligan tied him up as he did most nights so he could molest Avery."

Pullman's Adam's apple bobbed.

"He cut himself free, then went in to save Avery. But he claims Mulligan was already dead. That he thought Avery killed the old man, so he took a bloody knife from her hand, wiped it off, then stabbed Mulligan to cover for her."

Pullman fiddled with his suit jacket again. "You believe that story?"

"Yes," Avery said. "I remember a little more now. The window in my bedroom was open, and I heard a woman's voice. I think someone else was there."

Pullman looked confused. But he stood, went to a filing cabinet and removed a file. He flipped through it, then spread the crime scene pictures across his desk.

Avery had seen them before, but the gruesome sight of Mulligan's chest bleeding from the stabbing still turned her stomach.

Pullman tapped a finger on one of the pictures, then

shoved the report in front of Jaxon. "There was no second knife there, and no mention of it in the report."

Avery glanced at Jaxon, questions nagging at her. "Then someone took it."

"Or if police found it, they doctored the report," Jaxon suggested.

"You'd have to ask the officer who filed the report about that," Pullman said.

"Who called the police that night?" Jaxon asked.

Pullman scanned one of the pages. "All it says here is that a woman phoned 911 saying there was a disturbance at the house. When the police arrived, they found Mulligan dead with Hank standing over the body holding the bloody knife in his hand."

"Did anyone try to find out the identity of the female caller?" Jaxon asked.

Pullman shook his head. "Didn't seem important at the time."

Avery's heart raced. "Not important? What if that woman was in the house? She could have been the woman I heard in my room that night."

Jaxon snatched the report to look at it again. "Hell, Pullman, that was your case, your reasonable doubt. She could have killed the damn man herself, then called 911."

"I THOUGHT THAT Texas Ranger was supposed to keep things on track for the execution."

"He is."

"Well, hell, that's not what he's doing. He's trying to prove Tierney is innocent."

He muttered a string of expletives. "What?"

"Tierney's sister sucked him into believing her brother was all noble, some kind of hero protecting his little sister. And if he finds out about the second knife…"

"The second knife wasn't in the crime photos," he pointed out.

"No. But he's still digging." A heavy sigh escaped. "And he wants to know who called in the murder. He's going to try to make it look like the caller murdered Mulligan."

Dammit to hell and back. "What about my name?"

"I erased it from the police report just as you asked."

"Good. I don't want this cluster coming back to haunt me." Or screw up his career.

He'd worked too hard to build his reputation to go down now for putting away a punk like Hank Tierney.

Chapter Sixteen

Jaxon skimmed the police report again before he drove away from Pullman's office.

"Do you see anything else that can help Hank?" Avery asked.

Jaxon shrugged. "The officer who signed this report was named O'Malley. I'm going to call him and ask him some questions. But first, let's talk to the D.A."

Hope lit her eyes for a fraction of a second, making Jaxon want to promise her they'd save her brother.

But he didn't know if he could keep that promise.

As he drove, Avery seemed lost in thought, her emotion at having seen Hank obviously taking a toll.

He had a bad feeling about Pullman and the police report. Something wasn't right.

Either the second knife hadn't been found, or someone had removed it from the scene and intentionally covered up the fact that it had ever been there.

The only person who would do that was the real killer— or someone connected to him or her.

He parked, and together he and Avery walked up to the courthouse. They went through security, and then he escorted her to the D.A.'s office.

The man's reputation for being a cutthroat prosecutor was legendary in south Texas. From his first case as the assistant

D.A. when he'd tried Hank, William Snyderman had established himself as a winner who showed no sympathy for the criminals he put behind bars.

Jaxon knocked on the man's door and pushed it open when Snyderman called for him to come in.

Unlike Pullman, who looked shady, Snyderman was distinguished with close-cropped hair, gray at the temples, and a smile showcasing his confidence. He wore a designer suit, a red power tie and a black onyx signet ring encrusted with his initials in gold.

"I've been expecting to see you," Snyderman said as he extended his hand in greeting.

Of course, Director Landers would have relayed that he'd asked Jaxon to oversee the case.

Snyderman offered Avery a smile and his hand. "I'm sorry about your brother, Miss Tierney."

Avery bit down on her lip as she shook his hand. "I remember you," she said. "You're the reason my brother is on death row."

Snyderman squared his shoulders, a sharp glint in his eye. "Your brother is on death row because he murdered a man."

"What if he didn't?" Avery countered. "What if he's innocent and you convicted the wrong person?"

Snyderman's jaw hardened. "You don't really believe that, do you, Miss Tierney?"

"Yes, I do," Avery said, standing her ground. "And I'm going to prove it."

Snyderman started to speak, but Jaxon threw a hand up to keep them from arguing. Snyderman's tongue was like a viper, and Jaxon didn't want Avery to get stung.

"I have a few details I'd like for you to clarify," Jaxon said.

Steel-gray eyes cut to Jaxon for a second before he gestured for them to sit down. Jaxon had seen his ironclad control in court, and watched as Snyderman adopted his lawyer persona.

"What details?" Snyderman asked.

Jaxon explained that Avery remembered the voice of a woman from that night, and that the window had been opened, indicating a third party might have come into the house and left. "Coupled with the fact that the call to 911 came from a female, it's possible it was the same person, and that that woman killed Mulligan."

"You really are grasping, aren't you?" Snyderman asked. "Have you seen the crime photos? There's a picture of Hank with blood all over him, his hand clenching the murder weapon."

"That's also a problem," Jaxon said. "You see, Hank admitted he took a kitchen knife with him to bed, and he used it to escape after Mulligan tied him up. He heard the man going into Avery's room and ran in to save her. There, he found her holding a knife. She was in shock, so he wiped it down and then stabbed Mulligan to cover up for her."

Snyderman leaned back in his seat, hands steepled as he studied Jaxon then Avery. "That's quite a story."

"It's true," Avery said.

Snyderman's eyebrow shot up. "If I remember correctly, a second knife wasn't found at the crime scene."

Jaxon rubbed a hand over his chin. "That's one thing that's bothering me," he said. "If there was a second knife, it would prove that another person had been in that house that night."

"Not necessarily," Snyderman said, always the devil's advocate. "You could argue that both Hank and Avery took knives earlier." He angled his head toward Avery. "It might even suggest that you two planned the murder together."

Avery shot up from her seat, eyes glinting with fury. "We

didn't plan anything," she said. "Wade Mulligan beat Hank and molested me."

"There is your motive," Snyderman said, voice oozing confidence.

Avery crossed her arms. "Yes, we had motive, but so did other kids who'd lived there. One of them could have sneaked in that night and stabbed Wade."

"With you in the room?" Snyderman's voice screamed with disbelief. "And if that's the case, why wouldn't you have told the police that, Miss Tierney? If you believed your brother was innocent, why did you testify that he stabbed Mulligan?"

"I was just a child," Avery said in a tortured whisper. "I was frightened, and…traumatized by that night."

Jaxon fisted his hands by his sides. Snyderman was pointing out the obvious holes in their theory, the same way a judge or another attorney would.

But the bastard was wrong. He had to be.

Jaxon cleared his throat, adopting his own authoritative air. "Miss Tierney is not on trial, Snyderman. She was only nine at the time and in shock. You know from experience that children often repress traumatic memories, but years later when they reach adulthood, those memories resurface."

Snyderman sighed warily. "That may be true, but you've shown me nothing to make me believe that Hank Tierney was wrongly convicted."

Jaxon hated to admit it, but the D.A. was right. He had a decent theory but no concrete evidence, not even a specific suspect. Just conjecture.

He still didn't like the man's attitude toward Avery, though. "Just for a moment, consider the possibility that our theory is correct," Jaxon said. "If a third party, say this woman who called in the murder, sneaked in and killed Mulligan, she's gotten away all these years. Avery's scream must have prompted her to run, and the woman dropped the knife. The ME also confirmed that the actual fatal wound was made by a left-handed person, not a right-handed one. Hank Tierney is right-handed."

For the first time since they'd entered, unease flashed on Snyderman's face. But not for long. "A right-handed person could have used his left hand to inflict that wound to confuse police."

"Hank was fourteen, emotional, in a rage. I hardly think he had the presence of mind to make a decision like that."

Snyderman steepled his hands again. "But it's possible. He could have planned it while he was tied up in his room. Or hell, for days, for that matter."

Jaxon narrowed his eyes. "Did the police find ropes in Hank's bedroom? They should have, and the defense attorney should have made the argument of abuse."

Snyderman looked down at his hands. "I don't recall."

Jaxon didn't remember seeing them in the report or photos, either.

"But if there were ropes," Snyderman continued, "the police could have assumed Hank planned to use them to tie up Mulligan."

The man had an answer for everything.

Jaxon leaned forward, his gaze penetrating Snyderman. "You know, I believe the police did a shoddy job of processing this case. I know the defense attorney didn't do his job. And now I'm wondering if you didn't do yours, either."

Snyderman leaned forward as well, meeting Jaxon's gaze head-on, his eyes cold. "What are you implying, Sergeant Ward?"

Jaxon gritted his teeth. He could be about to kiss his career goodbye. But Avery was counting on him, and Hank Tierney might lose his life for doing nothing but protecting his little sister.

Jaxon couldn't live with that.

"I understand you built your reputation on this conviction," Jaxon said, forging ahead in spite of the warning in the D.A.'s eyes. "But maybe you, the police and the defense attorney were a little too eager to close this case."

Anger seared Snyderman's expression. "You're implying that the police removed evidence? That I acted with impropriety?"

"I don't know," Jaxon said. "But I'm going to talk to the officer who wrote that initial report. O'Malley, I think it was."

Snyderman grunted. "O'Malley died five years ago."

Damn, but Snyderman almost looked smug about the man's death.

And with O'Malley dead, how would they learn if someone had found that second knife?

He didn't like the other question nagging at him. Director Landers had made his career on this case, as well. Had he hidden or covered up evidence that could have cast doubt on Hank's guilt, maybe even exonerated him?

AVERY WAS SHAKING with anger and frustration as they left the D.A.'s office.

Just the sound of Snyderman's harsh voice had triggered memories of sitting in court twenty years ago. Of watching the faces of the jurors as he'd ranted about Hank's violent tendencies, about the number of times he'd stabbed Mulligan.

Then he'd plastered pictures of the bloody scene in her bedroom the night of the murder on a screen, and the women and men watching had gasped and whispered in shock.

The psychologist who'd treated her after the murder had tried to shield her from the sight of the photos, but she'd seen them anyway.

"Are you okay?" Jaxon asked.

No, she wasn't okay. How could she be? Time was running out, and she knew her brother was innocent but couldn't prove it.

"It's my fault. If I'd told the social worker about what Wade was doing, maybe she would have removed us from the home and none of this would ever have happened."

Jaxon cradled her hand in his. "We're not giving up yet, Avery. Let's talk to that social worker and see if she can shed some light on the situation."

She gripped his hand, taking comfort in the warmth of his fingers as he enclosed her smaller hand in his.

Thirty minutes later, they parked at Erma Brant's house, a small wooden-framed structure on a street lined with similar older homes.

"You worked with Delia," Jaxon said as they walked up the sidewalk to the door. "Did you ever meet Erma Brant?"

"I don't think so," Avery said. "But Hank and I did go through a couple of other social workers before Delia was assigned to us."

Jaxon knocked, and she glanced at the withered flowers and peeling paint on the house. The screens were torn, and the house needed a new roof.

Seconds later, a thin woman wearing a housedress and bedroom shoes opened the door. She squinted up at them over bifocals. "Yeah?"

"Mrs. Brant?" Jaxon said. "My name is Sergeant Jaxon Ward with the Texas Rangers. Can we talk to you for a minute?"

"You want Erma," the woman said in a high-pitched voice.

"Yes," Jaxon said.

"That's my sister. Come on in, she's in the kitchen."

They followed her through a cluttered foyer piled high with laundry, knickknacks and dozens of magazines, then found Erma Brant sitting in a wheelchair at a round oak table.

"Erma, it's one of them Texas Rangers," the sister shouted.

She made a sign with her hand to indicate Erma was hard of hearing.

Erma looked at Jaxon with a scowl, then glanced at Avery. "My God, you're Hank Tierney's sister, aren't you?"

Avery nodded. "You remember me?"

Erma's lip quivered as she took a sip of tea. "Didn't really know you and your brother, but I saw your pictures in the news. They've been showing it again, what with the execution coming up."

"That's the reason we're here," Jaxon said. "Erma, there's some new information that's come to light, and we need your help. We now know that Wade Mulligan was abusing Hank and Avery."

Avery watched for shock on the woman's face, but her expression went flat. "Who are you?"

"Avery Tierney," Avery said.

Erma suddenly looked confused and glanced at her sister. "What are they doing here? Where's Mama?"

The sister rushed over and patted Erma's back, then gave Avery and Jaxon a wary look. "I'm sorry, I should have warned you. Erma has some memory problems."

"Alzheimer's?" Jaxon asked.

The sister nodded. "Started about ten years ago. She has good days and bad days. Sometimes she remembers details of things that happened years ago but can't remember my name or her own."

"Get these people some tea," Erma said. "I should have made my shortcakes."

Despair tugged at Avery. How could Erma help them if her memories were faulty?

Jaxon slipped into the chair across from Erma. "Erma, you were telling us that you saw the story about Wade Mulligan being murdered on the news."

Erma's eyes widened. "Yes, that was horrible. They say those kids that lived with him killed him."

Avery tensed. "Did you know that Wade was hurting the little girl and boy?"

Erma's hand trembled so hard the teacup rattled against the saucer. "I got Imogene out of there."

"You did?" Avery asked. But not before she'd been totally traumatized.

Jaxon lowered his voice. "Did you report the abuse to the police?"

Erma set down the teacup. "I told one of them. He said he talked to the couple, but they claimed the kids were lying."

Erma stood and walked to the window, then picked up a doll in the corner and began to rock it in her arms. "Shh, baby, don't cry," Erma whispered. "Mama's right here."

Avery glanced at Jaxon and saw the frustration on his face. They were losing Erma again.

"I'm sorry," the sister said. "When she shuts down, she shuts down."

Erma sank into the rocking chair and began to hum and stroke the doll as if it were a child.

Jaxon addressed the sister. "Did Erma ever talk to you about the Mulligans or the Tierney arrest?"

"No, not really. Although she was upset about all the children placed with the Mulligans. She said she felt sorry for them." Erma's sister fiddled with the collar of her blouse. "When she reported Imogene's abuse and the police didn't do anything, she said she was going to quit work, that she couldn't do her job anymore."

"So she left social work?" Jaxon asked.

Erma's sister nodded. "Said she was going to leave a note in the files for the person who filled her position, a note telling them not to put any more children in the Mulligan house."

Avery froze. Had Erma left a note in the file? If so, why hadn't Delia mentioned it?

And what if Erma had discovered that she and Hank had been placed with the Mulligans against her advice?

She looked at the frail, unstable woman in front of her. She was confused now. But she was whispering to the baby doll that everything would be all right.

Just as the woman had whispered to Avery the night of the murder.

Dear God, had Erma come to check on her and Hank? Had Erma sneaked in and whispered to her that everything would be all right?

She'd been burned out on the job. She was upset with the police for not believing her, for not stopping Mulligan.

What if she'd been angry enough to kill Mulligan so he couldn't abuse any more children?

JAXON LISTENED TO Avery's theory as they drove back to her house.

"I need to talk to Delia again," Jaxon said. "Find out why she said she didn't see the note Erma left in the files requesting that the Mulligans not be used as a foster family again."

Avery grabbed one of the boxes holding her brother's mail and carried it to the house. He snagged the other two boxes and followed her.

But his phone buzzed as she started to open the door. He checked the number.

Director Landers. Probably going to fire his butt.

"Let me take this," he said, then stepped to the edge of the porch.

Avery went inside and closed the door, and he saw a light flip on. He punched the director's number, bracing himself.

A second later, Avery's scream pierced the air.

Jaxon's heart clenched as he shoved his phone in his pocket, reached for his gun and rushed to the door.

Chapter Seventeen

Avery swung her elbow backward and jabbed her attacker in the stomach. He tightened his grip.

"Be still," the man growled. "I'm not going to hurt you."

Old fears crawled inside her, memories of Mulligan's attacks, and she screamed and stomped on his foot as hard as she could, using self-defense moves she'd learned in a class at the gym. He bellowed again, then shoved her toward the chair in the living room.

She fell into it, hands reaching out to catch her from bouncing off and hitting the floor.

"Damn, Avery, I'm here to help!"

Avery froze, the man's rough voice resurrecting some distant memory from the past. Gasping for a breath, she pushed up from the chair with her hands and turned to face him.

Dark shadows hovered around his silhouette, but she could tell he was big. Over six feet. Broad shouldered.

And he was clutching his belly and breathing hard.

"Freeze—police!" Jaxon shouted as he crept up behind her attacker.

Avery's lungs strained for air as she cried out.

The man spun around and kicked Jaxon's gun from his hand, sending it sailing across the floor.

Avery struggled to see the intruder's face, but suddenly Jaxon lunged onto the man's back.

Avery clenched the chair edge as Jaxon knocked him to the floor. Jaxon jumped him and tried to jerk his arms behind him, but the man shoved him, then rolled over and slammed his fist into Jaxon's jaw.

Jaxon grunted and punched him in the stomach, and they traded blows, rolling across her floor as they fought.

"Get off me!" the man shouted.

"You son of a bitch, you're not going to hurt Avery," Jaxon growled.

"I'm not trying to," the man yelled.

Avery's heart pounded, but she turned on the lamp by the chair. A soft light washed over the room, and she stared in shock at the man lying on the floor with Jaxon straddling him.

"Jaxon, stop," she whispered.

He swung his gaze up toward her, his eyes feral. "What?"

Avery stood on shaky legs, walked over and looked down at the man. It had been over twenty years since she'd seen him.

His face was weathered, wrinkled, and age spots dotted his bald head.

But she would never forget his face or those twisted eyes.

"Avery?" Jaxon said.

"Tell him to let me go," the man growled.

Jaxon jerked the man by the collar.

"It's okay, Jaxon," Avery said. "You can release him. He's Roth Tierney, my father."

JAXON SHOT THE man below him a sinister look. He could feel Avery trembling beside him. "You're Avery's father?"

The bald man grunted a yes.

Jaxon cursed. "Then why the hell did you break in and attack her?"

"I just wanted to talk to her." He gestured at Jaxon's hands, which were still planted firmly on the man's chest where he was sitting on him to hold him down. "Now let me up."

Jaxon glanced at Avery and saw the bewilderment and hurt on her face, firing his anger even more. "Just don't touch her again," he warned.

The beefy man's eyebrows shot up, but Jaxon ignored them. As far as he knew, Avery's old man hadn't been part of her life in years. And he was the reason she and her brother had ended up in foster care in the first place.

But he yanked the man by his collar, then climbed off him and moved to stand beside Avery. He planted his feet firmly in place, arms folded, daring the man to approach her.

No one was ever going to hurt Avery again.

Avery's raspy breathing punctuated the silence as her father stood. Time had been rough on him. His hands were scarred, a prison tattoo wound across his wrist, his teeth were crooked and yellowed, his hair was gone and he had a paunch.

"What are you doing here, Dad?" Avery asked in a frosty tone.

He brushed off his jeans with his hands. "We need to talk."

Jaxon cleared his throat and pointed to the sofa. While Tierney walked over and took a seat, he retrieved his gun and stowed it in his holster. Avery claimed the club chair in front of the fireplace, but Jaxon remained standing.

His instincts were on full alert.

"I thought you were still in prison," Avery said.

Tierney shook his head. "I've been out awhile."

"How long?" Jaxon asked.

Tierney knotted his scarred hands on his thighs. "Since right before Hank went to jail."

Shock flashed on Avery's face. "What?"

Tierney studied her for a long moment, then glanced at

Jaxon, the air thick with tension. "I've been out," he said. "Well, in and out a few times over the past twenty years."

Avery's look flattened. "What do you want? If it's money, I don't have any."

"I don't want money," he said. "I came to help you."

Jaxon scrutinized him. "How do you plan to do that?"

Tierney hissed between his teeth. "Look, Avery, I know you and Hank got sent to foster care 'cause of me, 'cause I killed that man. I screwed up."

"You tore our family life apart," Avery said bitterly.

"I know," Tierney said. "And when I got out on parole, I came looking for you and Hank. I found out you were at the Mulligans and I went there and watched you get on the school bus, watched you and Hank outside."

Jaxon wondered where this was going.

"You watched us?" Avery asked, her voice laced with unease.

"Yeah." Tierney dropped his head forward and studied his blunt nails. "I saw what he was doing to you," he mumbled. "I knew it was my fault. I…wanted to stop him."

Disbelief registered on Avery's face.

"What did you do?" Jaxon asked.

Tierney raised his head and looked at Avery, then at Jaxon. A vein throbbed in his forehead. "I broke in the damn house and stabbed the creep."

Jaxon narrowed his eyes. "You killed Mulligan?"

Tierney nodded, then held out his hands, wrists pressed together in surrender. "You can arrest me now, Sergeant Ward."

AVERY'S HEAD WAS reeling from seeing her father again. And here he was, after being absent from her life for twenty years, turning himself in for Wade Mulligan's murder?

She didn't know what to believe.…

Jaxon wrangled a pair of handcuffs from his jacket pocket

and snapped them around her father's wrists. She wasn't sure what he was thinking, if he believed her father, but he looked more than happy to handcuff him.

Mixed emotions pummeled Avery. She wanted to free Hank more than anything. Her father's arrest might make that possible. She certainly didn't have any emotional attachment to the man. "If you killed Wade Mulligan, why didn't you come forward sooner? Why did you let Hank go to prison for life?"

Tierney's nostrils flared. "Because the stupid boy confessed, and stabbed Mulligan a bunch of times. I…thought maybe he inherited my bad genes, and that he needed to do a little juvy time to straighten him up." A hefty amount of regret darkened his face. "I never thought he'd be convicted."

"But he was convicted and is going to be put to death this week," Avery cried, heart sick that her father would stand by and let Hank suffer. "For heaven's sake, Hank confessed because he thought I killed Wade Mulligan. He was only protecting me."

Shock registered on her father's eyes. Then a string of curse words exploded.

"How could you do that to us?" Avery whispered in a raw voice. "I lost everything that day, and so did Hank."

He grunted. "I figured he'd do a little time and then they'd let him out. I never expected him to get the death sentence."

"But when they gave it to him, why didn't you come forward then? Why wait until a few days before the execution?"

"I know it was wrong, but I'm here now." Emotions glittered in her father's eyes, maybe true remorse; then he tightened his jaw and faced Jaxon. "You can take me in now, Sergeant Ward. I'll confess to everything, and then you can get my son free."

JAXON WASN'T CONVINCED Tierney was guilty. His appearance at this late date seemed too…coincidental. Any lawyer would argue that he'd only come forward to save his son from dying.

Then again, if Jaxon could use his confession to get a stay, it would give him more time to investigate and unearth the truth.

Anguish filled Avery's eyes. Damn. He wanted to sweep her in his arms and comfort her. But Tierney shoved up from the chair, his expression hard as he gestured toward the door.

"Let's go, Sergeant. Sooner we get this over with, sooner you can get my boy out of prison."

Jaxon's dark gaze met the man's, searching for the truth.

He needed to learn more about Tierney's prison behavior. What other crimes he might have committed since he said he'd been released.

And why had he been released?

Hell, if he were lying and taking the blame for his son, it was probably the first noble thing he'd ever done in his life.

And Jaxon didn't intend to stop him. Avery and Hank deserved help, and it was about time their loser old man stepped up.

"Mr. Tierney, you are under arrest for the murder of Wade Mulligan. You have the right to remain silent..." He read Tierney his Miranda rights as he escorted him outside to his SUV.

Avery followed him, her arms wrapped around herself, her breathing choppy.

"Stay here and lock the doors," he said. "I'll call you."

She shook her head. "No. I'm going with you."

Jaxon ground his teeth, but the determined look on Avery's face warned him not to argue. Hell, how could he blame her?

She hadn't seen her father in two decades, and now he'd confessed to the murder that had sent her brother to death row. If it were his family, he'd insist on being present to see what happened.

"Wait on me, Jaxon. Let me lock up and grab my coat."

He gave her a clipped nod. "I'll be right here."

Her eyes softened as if she realized he meant that on more than one level.

And he did. Hell, he wanted to erase the pain in those damn gorgeous eyes of hers, and make her smile.

But tonight was bound to be rough. And they had their work cut out for them to convince a judge to postpone the execution.

Worry knitted her brow as if she realized the same thing, then she ran back toward the house.

Jaxon shoved Tierney into the backseat, then leaned across him to buckle his seat belt. "You'd better not be messing with Avery," he said in a lethal voice. "You've hurt her enough already."

Tierney lifted his head, his bald head pulsing red with anger. For a brief second, his gaze connected with Jaxon's, though, and Tierney's eyes flashed with understanding.

"I'm not here to hurt her," he said in an equally low, lethal tone. "For the first time in my life, I'm trying to do the right thing."

Whether he meant he was telling the truth about the murder or just trying to save his children, Jaxon didn't know.

He didn't care.

He climbed into the front, waited until Avery joined him, then started the engine and drove toward the jail.

Traffic was minimal as he passed through Cherokee Crossing. Most of the residents had settled in for the night, although the cantina was hopping with live music and the diner was still full with the late night supper crowd.

Avery twisted her hands in her lap, obviously grappling with emotions. Her father sat ramrod straight, staring out the window with a resigned look on his face. He'd been down this road before.

Prison was nothing new. Hell, sometimes lifers were released and didn't know what to do with themselves.

The system didn't prepare them for life on the outside. And society wasn't exactly jumping to employ ex-cons. Without a family member or friend providing support and a place to live, they wound up frustrated and failing.

Some even resorted to petty crimes to violate parole so they could go back to jail and have three square meals a day and a place to sleep.

Avery tugged her shawl around her as they got out, and he opened Tierney's door and escorted him inside. Deputy Kimball looked up from the front desk with a frown.

"Deputy, this is Roth Tierney, Hank Tierney's father. He just confessed to the murder of Wade Mulligan."

Jaxon's phone buzzed, and he checked the caller ID. Dammit—Director Landers.

"Book him and put him in an interrogation room. I need to answer this call. Then we'll take his statement."

Deputy Kimball grabbed Tierney's arm and led him through a set of swinging doors. Avery sank into the chair across from the deputy's desk, her face ashen.

Jaxon stepped outside for a moment and punched the director's number.

"What the hell is going on?" Director Landers bellowed. "Snyderman called and said you're trying to prove Hank Tierney is innocent."

Jaxon swallowed hard. "I reviewed all the evidence, and I had questions. But there is a problem, Director."

The director's hiss punctuated the air. "What?"

"Hank Tierney's father showed up and confessed that he killed Wade Mulligan."

The director spewed a dozen curse words. "You'd better put a lid on this right now, Ward. If Tierney's conviction is questioned, it could cast doubt on every case Snyderman and I worked for the past twenty years."

He didn't need another reminder.

But could he drop the case without knowing the truth?

Jaxon glanced through the window and saw Avery tracing that scar around her wrist, and he knew the answer.

He'd risk his job, his life, everything to save her from any more pain. And he would find the truth no matter what happened to him afterward.

Chapter Eighteen

Avery twined her hands together as she settled on the bench in the front room of the sheriff's office, her thoughts jumbled. She felt just as nervous as she had when she was called to the principal's office as a child.

Or worse—the way she had the day she sat outside the courtroom with that psychologist waiting to learn her brother's fate.

That day had ended in disaster and had shredded what was left of her trust in people. And in the system.

Would this day end as badly?

She mentally replayed the conversation with her father at her house, but anxiety needled her.

Had her father really broken in and killed Wade Mulligan?

If so, how had he gotten in without her seeing him?

She distinctly remembered hearing a woman's voice whisper to her that everything would be all right. Not a man's.

Although she had been afraid of Mulligan and had hidden under the covers, had repressed memories of most of that night. Maybe her father had been there.

If he'd broken into her room, she would have been frightened by him. She hadn't seen him since she was four years old, when he'd been incarcerated. She probably wouldn't have even recognized him.

And a big man climbing in her bedroom window in the dark would have terrified her.

She closed her eyes, desperately pressing her brain to recall more details....

The window screeched open, the wind was blowing, she was cold, so cold she was shaking. She heard his footsteps, heard Wade grumbling about Joleen being gone, smelled cigarette smoke and whiskey...

Knew he was coming for her.

Her skin crawled, and nausea rolled through her. Then she heard Hank yelling at Wade...heard Wade's fist slamming into Hank. Hank's grunt of pain. But Hank wasn't giving up.

He was strong and tried to take care of her. But Wade was big and mean, and he always got what he wanted.

She clenched the sheets, wishing she had some way to fight off Wade. She should have put Hank's baseball bat under her bed. Maybe she'd get it tomorrow. But that wouldn't help her tonight.

Hank shouted at Wade, but he must have tied him up because Wade's footsteps thundered in the hall. Then he burst through her door.

She squinted through the dark and saw his big shadow. Smelled him again.

She thought she was going to be sick. Then he moved toward her....

She screamed but...then everything went dark. Muffled sounds followed. Someone moving. A low voice. A grunt.

A thump. Wade falling?

She was shaking all over. Heard a moan. Wade...

A whisper brushed near her ear. "It'll be all right now...."

A woman's voice. Not her father's.

Then a hand touched her. Soft. Gentle.

The wind swirled cold air through the room. She tugged the quilt down and saw red, red everywhere. Blood...

Wade was on the floor, not moving. She had to get to Hank. She vaulted from the bed and ran toward Wade, had to get past him.

But just as she made it to him, his hand snaked out and grabbed her ankle. She froze, looked down and screamed at the blood on his chest. His eyes were wide, whites bulging, blood oozing from his mouth.

He jerked her foot and tried to drag her to the floor. Terrified, she spotted the knife and she reached for it....

The door to the front office opened, and Avery jerked her eyes open. Jaxon stood in the doorway, his expression guarded.

She started to say something, but what more could she tell him? She still believed a woman had been in her room. She didn't remember her father at all....

But she did remember picking up that knife.

Only it was bloody, and Wade was injured before she picked it up. Meaning she hadn't killed him.

Relief surged through her at that realization, although she still didn't know the truth.

Because if her memory of that woman was real, the woman killed Wade, not her father.

Jaxon strode into the sheriff's office, knowing he might be about to kiss his career goodbye. But the truth—and Avery—meant more to him than the job.

Odd—he'd never felt that way before. Had never thought he would.

But he couldn't abandon his integrity. If he did, he'd completely lose himself.

"Where did you go?" Avery asked.

"I had a phone call. I'll take your father's statement now."

Avery nodded, although he couldn't help thinking she looked like a confused, lost child sitting on that bench.

"Can I come with you?"

Jaxon shook his head. "An attorney could argue that your presence affected your father's statement."

"I see. All right."

"Do you want some coffee or something while you wait?"

She shook her head. "Thanks, though."

She was so polite and humble it aroused tender feelings inside him.

No one had ever taken care of her.

He wanted to change that.

A dangerous place to be, Ward.

Forcing himself back in professional mode, he strode through the double doors to the back and found Deputy Kimball guarding the door to the interrogation room.

"You want me in there?" the deputy asked.

Jaxon hesitated. He didn't, but it would probably be best to have confirmation that he'd handled the interrogation by the book. He didn't intend for the confession to get thrown out on a technicality. "You have cameras?"

The deputy shook his head. "No, but I have a recorder."

"Good. Set it up."

Jaxon opened the door, bracing himself in case Tierney had suddenly changed his story, but the big man looked calm, resigned. Determined. He was staring at his blunt nails again, his handcuffed hands splayed on the table.

"We're going to tape this interrogation," Jaxon said as Deputy Kimball set up the tape recorder. "All right with you, Tierney?"

His cold eyes stabbed Jaxon. "I figured you would."

"All right, then." Jaxon gave a brief introduction for the taping purposes. "This is Sergeant Jaxon Ward, Texas Ranger. Also present is Deputy Kimball from the Cherokee

Crossing Sheriff's Department. We are here to interview Mr. Roth Tierney."

He recited the date and time. "Now, Mr. Tierney, tell us exactly what happened the night Wade Mulligan was murdered."

Tierney heaved a big breath. "When I got outta prison, I looked up the kids. But when I tried to see them, the social workers told me no. And my probation officer warned me not to go near them."

Jaxon frowned. "Why?"

"He said I needed to prove myself first. Get a job. A decent place to live." He worked his mouth from side to side. "Like going through the proper channels ever worked for me or did my kids any good."

Jaxon resisted a comment. "Go on."

"I found out Hank and Avery were living at the Mulligans', and I drove by the house." He rubbed a hand over his eyes. "I just wanted to see them, make sure they were okay."

"*Did* you see them?"

Tierney nodded. "Just glimpses. I watched them get on the bus to go to school. Walk to the store. I…couldn't believe how big my boy was, but I could tell he had an attitude. He looked like I did at that age. Full of rage."

"And Avery?"

The man chewed the inside of his cheek for a minute. "I never seen anything prettier in my life. Reminded me of her mama before she got messed up on drugs and ran off."

Jaxon bit back a retort. "Did you talk to her?"

Tierney shook his head. "I figured she hated me. I know they told her what I done, and figured I needed to clean up first. But—" he hesitated "—I knew something was wrong. She looked so sad, and she had bruises on her legs."

Jaxon grimaced. "What did you do then?"

"I was still trying to do the right thing, didn't figure I'd do the kids any good if I ended up back in prison. But

I couldn't get those bruises out of my mind, so that night I drove by again. I parked in front of the house. Then I heard screaming." He made a low sound in his throat. "I couldn't let that bastard hurt her anymore, so I went up to the window and looked in. That's when I saw Mulligan sneaking into Avery's room." His cheeks reddened with anger, and he balled his hands into fists. "I ain't no fool. I did time. I knew what that SOB was doing to my little girl." He banged his fists on the table. "I had to stop him. So I sneaked in the window and killed him."

Jaxon waited for him to elaborate, but Tierney leaned back in the chair as if he were finished.

Dammit, Jaxon had to do his job and ask for more details.

Police received false confessions all the time. Mentally unstable folks, delusional ones, or some just wanting to take credit for a crime for attention.

Others did so to cover for someone else.

The key to discerning whether or not the confession was real lay in the details.

Police usually omitted facts from the news to help them later weed out the phonies and pinpoint the right perpetrator.

"How did you kill him?" Jaxon asked.

Tierney heaved a breath. "I stabbed him."

"Did you have a knife with you?"

Tierney hesitated. "No. I grabbed a kitchen knife when I went inside and used it."

Jaxon studied him. Tierney could have learned that from the news report. "Where exactly did you stab him?"

Tierney's mouth twitched with anger. "In the chest, where else? I wanted to kill the jerk."

"How many times did you stab him?" Jaxon asked.

For a moment, Tierney looked away, as if he didn't intend to answer.

"How many times?" Jaxon asked.

"Once. Went straight through the heart. Learned that in prison. Fastest way to kill someone is to aim for a main artery."

"Then what did you do?"

The man's mouth twitched again. "I threw the knife down. Avery was on the bed screaming and I panicked. I didn't want to get caught, so I rushed outside. I figured Hank would call the police and they'd think there was an intruder, and then Avery and Hank would go back to social services. Then I might get them back."

"But that didn't happen," Jaxon said, stating the obvious.

Tierney shook his head. "Hell, no, Hank had to go in and stab the bastard a bunch of times, then tell everyone he killed Mulligan."

Disgust ate at Jaxon. "Why didn't you come forward and admit the truth then?"

Tierney locked eyes with him. "I seen the meanness in my boy's eyes. I figured he needed some cooling-off time. I never thought they'd sentence him to death row."

Jaxon crossed his arms. "But they did, and you've had plenty of time to confess before now."

Tierney's cuffs clanged against the table. "Truth is, I went on a bender after that night. Lasted a few weeks. Then I wound up back in prison for violating parole. By then, the trial was over and Hank had been sent away."

Jaxon still didn't know if Tierney was telling the truth. But if his confession cast doubt on Hank, he could use it.

So he shoved a pad in front of the man. "Write down everything you just told me."

Tierney grabbed the pen, then picked up the pad Jaxon had laid on the table and began to write.

A knot seized Jaxon's belly. The stab wound to the aorta had been made by a man holding a knife with his left hand.

Tierney was right-handed.

BY THE TIME Jaxon emerged from the back, Avery thought she was going to pull her hair out. She'd already bitten her fingernails down to the nubs.

She stood, anxious to hear what he had to say, but his expression was unreadable.

"Deputy Kimball is securing your father in a cell for the night," Jaxon said. "I need to make a couple of calls, and then I'll drive you back to your house."

Jaxon stepped outside again, and she paced, wondering if she should ask to see her father. But bitterness swelled inside her. What could she possibly have to say to him?

Thanks for finally coming forward? Thanks for trying to save me twenty years ago?

Thanks for letting Hank rot in a cell when you could have spoken up years ago and my brother might have had a life?

Jaxon returned a moment later, his mouth set. "I left a message with my director and the judge explaining the turn of events."

"What happens next?" Avery asked.

"We'll contact the governor to grant a stay for Hank."

Hope jolted through Avery. Was it really going to happen?

Would they free her brother? Would she and Hank finally get a chance to be a family again?

Chapter Nineteen

"Thank you, Jaxon."

A tense heartbeat passed before he acknowledged her words. "Let's go."

She glanced at the door leading to the back rooms, but old hurts and shame mushroomed inside her, overriding her need to see her father. If he'd really loved her, he would have stuck around that night and made sure she and Hank were safe.

He should have been there for both of them at the trial, as well.

But he'd abandoned them and caused them to suffer for most of their life. How could she possibly forgive him for that?

Jaxon seemed distracted as he drove her back to her house. When they arrived, he parked and followed her up to the door.

"Thanks for tonight," Avery said.

"I'm coming in."

"But my father is locked up."

"He may have killed Mulligan, but he didn't leave you threats or paint nasty words on your house."

Avery's stomach clenched. She'd forgotten about the vandalism.

"I still think the key to the threats may be in the mail Hank received at the prison."

"We can look over everything tonight."

"I'll do it while you go to bed," Jaxon said. "You've got to be exhausted, Avery."

It had been a traumatic day. But for the first time in years, she had hope that her brother might be released, and that she might have some kind of family again.

All thanks to Jaxon.

"I'm sure you're tired, too," she said softly. "Maybe we can look at those letters tomorrow."

Jaxon shook his head. "No, I want to review them tonight."

She reached up to touch him, but he stepped away. "Go to bed, Avery."

Hurt stabbed her. Before when he'd kissed her, she'd thought he might have felt something.

But she'd obviously imagined the attraction because she had no experience with men.

So she retreated to the bathroom to get ready for bed alone.

WORRY STILL NAGGED at Jaxon as he watched Avery head into the bedroom. Convincing the judge that Tierney's confession hadn't been fabricated because of a last-ditch attempt to overturn Hank's conviction was going to be damn hard.

He didn't want to burst Avery's bubble that he might not be able to pull it off.

Especially if he pointed out that her father was right-handed, and they believed the real killer had inflicted the wound with his left hand.

Dammit, if only they had prints to match or some other piece of concrete evidence to point to the real murderer.

He made a makeshift desk on Avery's kitchen table, then took the first box of Hank's mail and began to sort through it.

He skimmed through each letter, noting the tone, and

divided them into categories—sympathetic letters stating views against the inhumane treatment of prisoners and the death sentence, personal letters from women who'd read Hank's story or seen his picture and wanted to meet him. Others offered conjugal visits and the occasional marriage proposal. Some pro–death penalty people claimed that an eye for an eye was the appropriate punishment. Religious zealots also promised to pray for his soul to be saved so he could enter Heaven.

The past few weeks Hank's mail had increased exponentially due to the publicity about the upcoming execution. He quickly read through the people's reactions and comments.

But one letter caught his attention, and made him pause. He read it a second time, trying to discern the underlying meaning—if there was one.

Dear Hank,

I'm so sorry that you spent your life in prison, and have prayed for you every day for the past twenty years. You were a lost, angry boy, and you had reason to be angry.

I wish I could change the outcome of that night for you. But I know you hated Wade Mulligan, and he deserved to die for what he did to you and your sister.

Mistakes were made back then. The Mulligans never should have been allowed to have children in their home. I'm so sorry that you and Avery were hurt by them.

At least Wade's death saved other children from suffering the way you did.

I pray for your soul, and for forgiveness for my own.

Jaxon exhaled. There was no signature. But it certainly sounded as if the writer had known the situation in that house.

As if he or she felt guilty.

The verbiage also sounded like that of a woman.

Avery claimed she'd heard a woman's voice that night, a woman assuring her everything would be all right now.

He studied the names of all the females associated with the case.

Joleen could have killed her husband, except he didn't think she had the courage. And she certainly hadn't appeared to harbor guilt over anything, not enough to write an apology note for it.

Imogene Wilson had ranted that she'd killed Mulligan, but her mind was so fractured that her testimony wouldn't stand up in court. She also wouldn't have had the mental capacity to write Hank and apologize, either.

The same went for Erma Brant. At one time she might have had the presence of mind to kill Mulligan and regret the way it turned out for Hank. But this letter had been postmarked in the past six months. Erma had been suffering from dementia for years.

Lois Thacker, now a police officer, had been honest about the Mulligans' abuse, but she seemed too hardened to write a heartfelt letter like this. Of course, he hadn't spoken with her for long. As a cop, she would know how to cover herself and avoid suspicion.

He skimmed his notes again. Delia Hanover had been nice, worked with children and was sincerely sorry for Hank and Avery. But at the time, she was young and new on the job, and claimed she hadn't known about the abuse. He couldn't imagine her killing anyone, much less being devious enough to cover up a crime.

Who else?

A noise jarred him, and he stood and walked to the back porch door to look out. The wind whirled, snapping trees and sending tumbleweed across Avery's backyard. Shadows flickered in the woods, making him tense.

But he studied the thicket of trees and didn't see any movement.

The noise sounded again, and he walked back to the hall, then realized the sound was coming from Avery's bedroom.

His heart squeezed. What if someone had climbed through the back window?

He gripped the gun in his holster and peered into her room.

Moonlight streaked the walls and floor, a sliver of golden light dappling Avery's bed where she lay thrashing against the covers.

Another nightmare.

Hell. As much as he wanted to end this ordeal for her tomorrow, he still wasn't certain they had Mulligan's real killer in custody.

He started to close the door and leave her, but she cried out again, and his heart wrenched.

Maybe he didn't have all the answers tonight. But he could offer her some comfort.

Unable to resist, he eased inside and walked toward her bed. When he reached the side, she startled and opened her eyes.

"Avery?"

Seconds stretched, causing his heart to hammer.

Then she reached out her hand and beckoned him to come to her.

AVERY BLINKED JAXON into focus. His dark features were almost lost in the shadows, but she couldn't confuse his raw masculine scent with anyone else. Strength and courage emanated from him as he reached his hand out and took hers.

"You were having another nightmare," Jaxon said as he lowered himself onto the mattress beside her. He removed his holster and laid it and his weapon on the nightstand.

Her cheeks heated with embarrassment, but he was so

close that she breathed in his essence, and all embarrassment faded.

She was just a woman here, and he was a man. The dark room, moonlight and his quiet breathing seemed so intimate that she lost her inhibitions.

She'd never trusted anyone before, but she trusted Jaxon with her brother's life. With her life.

With her heart…maybe not. But close enough that she wanted to feel him next to her.

"Jaxon," she whispered. "Lie down with me. Hold me."

Wariness echoed in the next breath he took. "That's not a good idea, Avery."

Need and desire rippled through her. The fact that he was trying to be polite only made her want him more.

"Why not?" She reached up and tugged at his shirt collar. "I don't want to be alone."

He closed his eyes, his body tensing, but she ran a hand down his chest, then drew slow circles on his abdomen. He sucked in a sharp breath, then caught her hand in his.

"You're playing with fire, Avery."

A smile curved her mouth. She'd never been one to play games, to flirt. She didn't even know how.

But for once in her life she wanted to feel a man next to her. To touch him.

To be with him.

Instinctively she knew that Jaxon would never hurt her.

She licked her lips, hoping he wouldn't reject her as she lifted her finger and traced it along his lower lip. "I want to be with you, Jaxon."

He hissed between clenched teeth. "I'm trying to be noble, Avery. The last thing I want to do is take advantage of you."

She raised her head and flicked her tongue along his lips where her finger had just been. "You are noble. That's one reason I want you," she said in a husky whisper. "I need you."

A low groan rumbled from his throat, and then he slid his hands beneath her head and brought his mouth to hers. "Stop me anytime," he murmured.

"I won't," she said softly.

He lifted his head and looked into her eyes. His were dark with passion and hunger, but there was something else there. Control. A fierce determination that she believe him.

"I mean it," he said against her ear. "Anytime—"

"Shh." She kissed him tenderly. "I trust you." She threaded her fingers deep into his thick dark hair. "Please make love to me, Jaxon."

Emotions flashed on his face. Then he moaned again and claimed her mouth with his.

JAXON HAD FOUGHT his desire as long as he possibly could. Avery's soft plea turned him inside out. He wanted nothing more than to please her and chase away her bad dreams.

He gently traced his tongue along her mouth, tentatively at first, his body hardening as she parted her lips and invited him inside. Need drove him to deepen the kiss, and their tongues tangled in a sweet erotic dance unlike anything he'd ever experienced.

She moved against him, her hands pulling him closer, heat erupting between them as he stroked her hair away from her face. Her breath rushed out, her chest rising, breasts brushing his chest.

Her fingers slowly moved down to his back, clutching him, and he kissed her, then traced his tongue along the soft shell of her ear. She curled up against him, her hands growing urgent as she tugged at his shirt.

She was wearing a tank top and pajama pants, her nipples tightening below the thin material and making him ache for a taste.

She reached for his buttons and began unfastening them, their tongues dancing again as he helped her remove his shirt. She ran her hands over his bare chest, raking her fingers through the soft mat of dark hair on his torso.

"It feels good to touch you," she whispered.

A heady sensation shot through her, setting him on fire as her hand slid lower to his belt.

But he caught her hand and looked into her eyes again. "Avery?"

Pure feminine sex oozed from her eyes as she smiled. "You're going to force me to beg, Jaxon?"

The flirtatious tone to her voice made a laugh rumble from his chest. He'd wanted to pleasure her tonight, and she was smiling. There was so much more he could give her....

"I would never force you to do anything," he said, serious now.

"I know. Make me forget the past, Jaxon. Show me what it's like to be loved."

His gaze locked with hers. He was honored to have her trust. Heart pounding with the need to have her, he cradled her face between his hands again and kissed her once more, teasing her with frantic strokes until she moaned and lifted her hips into his.

His sex swelled and throbbed to be inside her.

Hungry to taste her, he slowly traced her nipples with his fingers through the thin tank, then kissed and suckled her neck, inching down to tease her nipples. She murmured a low sound in her throat and clutched his arms, silently asking for more.

Determined to please her, he lifted her tank, and she helped him peel it over her head. Her bare breasts were larger than he'd imagined, her nipples dark and stiff, enticing him to take them into his mouth.

He traced one with his fingertip while he closed his lips over the other. She cried out his name and ran her foot up his calf, teasing him. He laved both breasts, then inch by inch skimmed her pajama pants down her legs. The pair of see-through lacy white panties surprised him.

Her breath rasped out as he eased her legs apart and kissed her through the thin lace.

"Jaxon?"

"Let me have you," he whispered hoarsely.

She threw her head back and moaned as he tugged her panties down with his teeth, then teased her femininity with his tongue before he tasted her sweetness.

Chapter Twenty

Avery tingled all over from Jaxon's erotic ministrations. He lifted her hips and planted his tongue inside her, and she clenched the sheets, mind-numbing sensations spiraling through her.

He stroked her until she cried out his name and begged him to join his body with hers. Slowly he rose above her, rolled on a condom, then framed her face with his hands.

"Are you sure, Avery?"

"I've never been more certain of anything in my life."

Heat flared in his eyes as he nudged her legs apart and stroked her with his thick erection. She was moist and achy, her body begging for more, and she opened to him, welcoming him inside her as he gently entered her.

He paused, his arms shaking as he exerted control, giving her time to adjust to the feel of him. Hunger and passion drove her to pull his hips closer, and she moved against him in an urgent cry for him to go deeper.

Spurned by her encouragement, he moved his hips in a circular motion, thrusting deeper, inching out, then thrusting again. Erotic sensations shot through her, and soon they were tangled in each other's arms, bodies gliding against each other, kisses and tongues colliding as their lovemaking became more frantic.

Another orgasm began to build, the incessant throbbing

for more causing her to whisper his name, and he lifted her hips and filled her, his body jerking with his own release as her orgasm claimed her.

"I never knew it could be so beautiful," she whispered.

"Me, neither," he admitted gruffly.

They lay entwined, breathing unsteady, the heat between them rippling through her in the aftermath of their lovemaking. Who knew that touches and kisses could be so gentle and passionate? That they could feel so good, not hurtful?

That she would want Jaxon the way she had? The way she still wanted him?

Jaxon eased himself off her, then slid from bed and went into the bathroom. She suddenly felt bereft.

But he returned a moment later, slipped back into bed and pulled her into his arms.

"I'm glad you came back," she whispered.

His breath brushed her cheek. "I shouldn't have gotten in bed with you in the first place."

She shushed him, then cradled his face between her hands and kissed him. "You didn't enjoy it?"

"That's not what I meant." He nipped at her neck, then gently eased a strand of hair from her cheek. "You're beautiful, Avery. No matter what happens, don't forget that."

She stilled in his arms for a moment, wondering what he meant. Was he already pulling away?

Trying to warn her not to expect anything more from him?

Or warn her that he didn't think Hank would be freed?

He traced one finger down the slope of her breast, and she banished thoughts of Hank and her father and the investigation, and Wade Mulligan.

From this moment on, she would remember how it felt to have Jaxon's hands touching her, and no one else's.

Her heart stuttered, and she ran a hand over his hard chest, titillating sensations spiraling through her as he sucked in a sharp breath. The desire that heated his eyes emboldened her, and she crawled on top of him and kissed him again, naked skin against naked skin.

Then words were forgotten as they made love again. This time when her release spiraled through her, she bit back words of love, knowing Jaxon wouldn't want to hear them.

JAXON LEFT AVERY sleeping the next morning and showered, self-recriminations beating at him.

He hadn't made love to a woman in a while. Actually, he didn't know if he'd ever made love. He'd had sex before, but love was never involved. Neither was tenderness or the desperate kind of need he felt with Avery.

He'd certainly never slept all night with his partner, nor held her and loved her again and again.

He still wanted her.

Damn, emotional entanglements were dangerous. Avery might appear strong, but she'd been hurt badly before, and she was fragile.

Thankfully he kept a change of clothes in a duffel bag in his SUV in case he got stuck overnight on a case, and he dressed, then strapped on his gun and brewed a pot of coffee.

His phone buzzed, indicating a text, and he checked it. The director and the D.A. were going to meet him at the jail.

He started to scribble a note to Avery, but she appeared, her face flushed from their lovemaking, her eyes glittering with the memories.

His body hardened. In spite of his reservations, he wanted her again.

"I have to go to the sheriff's office," he said instead. "I'm meeting the D.A. and director of the FBI there."

Avery tightened the belt to her robe and poured herself a cup of coffee, although her hand trembled slightly. "I'll go with you."

"No." The word came out harsher than he'd intended, so

he tried to soften his reaction. "Stay here and shower. Rest. I'll call you when the meeting's over and let you know what happens."

"But this is about my brother," Avery said.

He didn't want to hurt her or disappoint her. And this meeting might not go well. "Please let me do my job and handle it."

Avery blew on her coffee. "All right. But promise you'll call me as soon as you can."

"I promise." He gestured toward the door. "Just keep the doors locked."

Avery nodded, and he put his mug in the dishwasher and headed out the door before he did something foolish like take her back to bed and admit that he loved her.

Dread for the upcoming meeting balled in his belly as he drove toward the jail. The director and the D.A. would be furious that Hank Tierney's father had come forward with a confession.

And could he present Tierney's confession to the judge knowing that it might not be legitimate?

Avery's face flashed in his mind, followed by Hank's tortured look. If he didn't, Hank might be put to death. And that would kill Avery.

But was he crossing the line by placing her feelings before the letter of the law?

AVERY CARRIED HER coffee to the table and saw the piles of letters Jaxon had sorted through. It took only a few minutes to understand the categories he'd organized them into.

She squinted to decipher his handwriting. He'd made several notes on a legal pad regarding the investigation and people they'd questioned.

Another letter lay separate from the pile, drawing her attention, and she picked it up and read it.

Dear Hank,

I'm so sorry that you spent your life in prison, and have prayed for you every day for the past twenty years. You were a lost, angry boy, and you had reason to be angry.

I wish I could change the outcome of that night for you. But I know you hated Wade Mulligan, and he deserved to die for what he did to you and your sister.

Mistakes were made back then. The Mulligans never should have been allowed to take children into their home. And I'm so sorry that you and Avery were hurt by them.

At least Wade's death saved other children from suffering the way you did.

I pray for your soul and for forgiveness for my own.

Avery's chest tightened. That letter…sounded like an apology. As if the person writing it knew that Hank was innocent.

Because the letter had been written by the real killer?

Not by her father, either. The handwriting was too feminine.

She glanced at the pad again. Jaxon had made a list of all the females they'd spoken with regarding Mulligan.

Two of the fosters, Imogene and Lois. The two social workers, Erma Brant and Delia Hanover.

Dear God, had one of them killed Wade?

And if so, what did Jaxon intend to do about her father?

Confusion and worry clawed at her, and she hurried to get dressed. Ten minutes later, she grabbed her purse and jacket and raced out the door.

Her father's confession taunted her as she barreled down the drive and onto the street leading into town. Had Jaxon decided the confession was bogus? That the woman in the letter killed Wade?

Was that the reason he hadn't wanted her to go with him today?

Pain wrenched her heart. She'd trusted Jaxon. Had given him her body and her heart. Did he have any feelings toward her?

She spun into the parking lot and climbed out, her nerves raw as she went inside. Jaxon's SUV was there, along with a black sedan.

But the front office was empty. Anxious, she opened the double doors to the back, pausing at the sound of loud voices.

Jaxon's. Then another man's.

She eased closer to the door, prepared to knock, but the man's words stopped her.

"Listen here, Ward, you were supposed to come here and make sure Hank Tierney's conviction wasn't questioned, not drum up another suspect that could make all of us who worked that case look like fools. And—" the man's voice rose "—I told you that if this case gets overturned, it'll mean every single case D.A. Snyderman or I worked will come under scrutiny. We're talking about hundreds of cases over the years."

Avery's chest constricted with hurt. Jaxon had come to Cherokee Crossing to make sure Hank was executed, not to find the truth.

But he'd pretended he wanted to help her. He'd lied to her and used her and...slept with her when he was working against her the entire time.

JAXON CHOKED BACK his anger. If he wanted to make a point with the director and D.A. Snyderman, he had to present a logical explanation.

"I understand your concerns," he said. "But as a lawman, I can't ignore the facts or that Hank recanted his confession."

"That boy was dangerous and deserved to go to jail," Snyderman said. "You saw how brutal he was in his attack."

"Hank Tierney was enraged because he was trying to protect his sister," Jaxon said through gritted teeth. "Tierney's lawyer should have used that in his defense. He should have called the social workers, other foster kids and teachers to testify that the children in that house were in danger."

"He got a defense," Snyderman said. "And all of us did our jobs back then."

The door swung open, and Jaxon jerked around to see Avery standing in the doorway glaring at all of them. "Did you do your jobs or did you railroad a frightened fourteen-year-old boy into prison?"

Jaxon opened his mouth to apologize, but Snyderman spoke up. "No one railroaded him into anything, Miss Tierney. Your brother confessed. He had the murder weapon in his hand and there were no other prints on it."

"Because he wiped them off to protect me!" Avery shouted.

Snyderman and the director exchanged concerned, nervous looks.

"You have no proof that your brother didn't kill Mulligan," Director Landers said.

Avery shot Jaxon a look of pure hatred. She'd obviously heard their conversation through the door and thought he'd betrayed her.

"What about my father's confession?" Avery asked.

Director Landers crossed his arms. "That will never hold up in court."

"It's obvious he's lying as a last attempt to save your brother," Snyderman said.

Avery turned to Jaxon. "Is that what you think, Sergeant Ward?"

The fact that she'd used his title and last name indicated

how upset she was. Dammit, he was caught between a rock and a hard place.

"Do you?" Avery cried.

Jaxon heaved a breath. He wanted to lie and protect her. He wanted to free her brother.

But his integrity won out. "I don't know," he said honestly. "You and I discussed the autopsy. The fatal wound was inflicted by a left-handed person."

Avery's brows rose, but resignation settled on her face. "And my father is right-handed."

He nodded.

"I'm left-handed," Avery said with a tilt to her chin. She faced Snyderman and the director. "I had the knife in my hand, and I had motive." She held out her arms. "Arrest me and set my brother free."

"Avery, stop it," Jaxon said. "Making a false confession is serious. I'm trying to unearth the truth once and for all."

"You're all trying to bury my brother." Tears glittered in Avery's eyes. "And that's not right."

Jaxon moved toward her, but she stepped back, her hand flying up in a warning for him not to touch her.

Then she turned and ran from the room. Jaxon started after her, but the director stepped in front of him. "Let her go, Ward. We're not finished here."

Jaxon stared at the director, his anger mounting. No, they weren't finished.

But he couldn't drop the case without finding the truth. He'd already lost Avery.

And he might lose his job.

But a man's life was at stake.

He would make sure justice was served, no matter who it hurt or what it cost him.

TEARS FLOODED AVERY'S eyes as she ran from the jail. She couldn't believe what a fool she'd been. That she'd trusted

Jaxon and opened herself up to him when he'd been working against her these past few days.

Although he had at least interviewed different people regarding the murder. That list of females on his pad at home flashed in her mind.

Which of those women were left-handed?

Not Joleen. Besides, she was too big a coward to have killed Wade.

And she definitely wasn't the kind of person to harbor enough guilt to write a heartfelt letter to Hank in prison.

Imogene was another possibility—but she was too unstable to testify about anything. The same with Erma.

Lois was a cop and could have been tough enough to kill Wade, even when she was young. She also could have decided to pay penance by becoming an officer who locked up others, like Wade.

Frustration made the tears come harder. Who else?

Delia Hanover, the woman who'd placed her and Hank in the home. She seemed nice, calm, caring. She worked with children now.

Avery struggled to recall if she was left- or right-handed and couldn't remember.

But Erma had said she'd written a note to the social worker who'd replaced her, advising her not to put children with the Mulligans.

Had Delia lied? Had she seen that note?

If so, why had she placed them in that house? Had she simply made a mistake?

What if there were foster children she and Jaxon had missed? Another female who'd been abused by Mulligan?

Delia would have access to those records. Avery started the car and sped toward the school. It was early morning and buses were just starting to run.

Maybe she could catch Delia before school started.

She punched the number for the school into her phone

and waited while it rang. When the receptionist answered, she asked for Delia.

"I'm sorry, but she called in sick today," the woman said.

"This is urgent. Can you tell me where she lives?"

"I'm sorry, but I'm not supposed to give out that information."

Avery thanked her and hung up, then pulled to the side of the road and did an internet search to find the woman's name. She found her address in seconds, and veered into a neighborhood of small wooden ranch homes.

Delia's car sat in the drive. Breathing out in relief, she parked and rushed up to the door. She knocked, praying Delia would have some answers that would help Hank. Another suspect.

The door opened and Delia appeared, her face ashen, her eyes dark.

"Delia, can we talk?"

Delia nodded and opened the door.

Then Avery saw the gun in the woman's hands.

Chapter Twenty-One

Jaxon berated himself for not handling the situation with Avery and his boss better.

Truthfully, Director Landers's attitude from the beginning had disturbed him.

"You know that Tierney's story has holes in it," Director Landers pointed out. "If he killed Mulligan, one of the kids would have seen him."

"He could have sneaked out before Hank came in the room," Jaxon said.

"But you said the fatal wound was made by a left-handed person," Snyderman said.

True. Jaxon's phone buzzed. The lab. "Let me take this."

He stepped aside and answered the call. "Sergeant Ward."

"This is Lieutenant Dothan. When we processed Ms. Tierney's house, I lifted some prints. I don't know if it means anything, but the print matched one we had in the system."

Jaxon clenched the phone tighter. "Whose was it?"

"A woman named Delia Hanover. She's a social worker—"

"I know who she is," Jaxon said, his chest tightening.

"Then it's not important?"

"It might be." Why would Delia's print be at Avery's house? Unless she had been the one to vandalize the place....

"Where did you find the print? What room?"

"The bedroom."

Jaxon's pulse hammered. "Thanks." He ended the call, his pulse spiking.

Director Landers cleared his throat. "Ward, this confession of Tierney's won't stand up."

Jaxon whirled on him. "You've wanted to bury this investigation to protect your career all along."

"I told you that reopening it would bring every case Snyderman and I worked into question."

Jaxon glared at both of the men. "What about the truth? The lab just called and said that a print was found at Avery's house when it was vandalized. That print belonged to the social worker who placed Avery and Hank in the Mulligan house." He folded his arms. "Someone tried to scare her away from investigating. I think that person was Delia Hanover."

Snyderman's face went pale, and he sank into the chair and scrubbed a hand down his chin. "Dear Lord."

A vein throbbed in Director Landers's forehead. "Why would she do that?"

"You know who she is, then?" Jaxon asked.

His boss scowled. "What difference does it make? Hank Tierney was convicted. He stabbed Mulligan numerous times. He was dangerous and we removed him from the streets."

"He was a fourteen-year-old boy who tried to save his little sister from being raped repeatedly by the man who was supposed to be taking care of him!" Jaxon bellowed.

Snyderman looked up at him grimly. "Hank Tierney was full of rage."

"He should have been," Jaxon said in a dark voice. "He was the only one protecting his sister."

"Delia tried," Director Landers said.

Jaxon swung his head back to his boss. "So you knew her?"

Director Landers looked shell-shocked for a moment as if he didn't realize he'd spoken.

"I…met her at the trial."

Snyderman cursed. "Give it up, Landers," he murmured. "It's time to tell the truth. Hank Tierney doesn't deserve to die, not if Mulligan was raping his sister."

"He was," Jaxon said.

"Tierney's lawyer should have done his homework," Snyderman said. "He should have brought up the abuse. But he was just a young punk overloaded with cases. And Hank's confession pretty much made the case."

"Because no one wanted to dig any deeper into the ugliness of the system," Jaxon muttered.

"That wasn't it," Director Landers said, his voice tinged with anger. "We were all young and ambitious and we wanted to do the right thing."

"The right thing would have been to find the truth, not lock up an innocent kid for trying to save his sister from a damned pedophile."

Snyderman grunted. "We thought Hank Tierney was dangerous," he said in a low voice.

Jaxon arched a brow. "But you knew he didn't kill Mulligan?"

A tense silence stretched between them; then Jaxon pounded his fist on the table. "Tell the truth once and for all, dammit. What happened?"

"Delia…" Director Landers began. "She was young, enthusiastic. It was her first job. She really cared about helping kids."

"Then you knew her personally, not just from the trial?"

Landers dropped his head into his hand with a groan. "Yes, we were dating," he admitted. "A few weeks after Delia placed the Tierney kids with the Mulligans, she found a note from the previous social worker."

"Erma Brant said she left a note advising against placing any more children with the Mulligans."

Director Landers gave a clipped nod. "Somehow the

note got lost. When Delia found it, she freaked out. She was terrified."

"Hadn't she been to the Mulligans' for a follow-up visit?" Jaxon asked.

Landers shook his head. "She was swamped with cases, and hadn't had time. But that night…she drove over." He sank into the chair and drummed his fingers on the table.

Jaxon tapped his foot impatiently. "Go on."

"When she arrived, she heard Avery screaming. Hank and Mulligan were going at it. She looked in the window and saw the old man tying Hank to the bed."

Jaxon swallowed back his disgust.

"What happened next?"

Director Landers sighed. "You have to understand. She didn't go over there to hurt Mulligan or kill him. But when she saw him go into Avery's room and realized what he was doing, she blamed herself. She panicked, grabbed a kitchen knife and ran in to stop him. He turned to fight her, and she stabbed him in self-defense."

"Then she whispered to Avery that everything would be all right," Jaxon said.

Landers nodded gravely.

"But instead of calling the police and explaining, she ran," Jaxon concluded, mentally putting together the pieces. "And when Hank freed himself, he went in and saw Avery. She was traumatized from witnessing the crime, had picked up the knife and crawled back in bed. He thought she stabbed Mulligan, so he took the knife from Avery, wiped her prints off, effectively wiping off Delia's, then stabbed Mulligan repeatedly. The police rushed in, and he confessed to cover for Avery."

Landers nodded again, his expression torn. Snyderman remained silent, a muscle ticking in his jaw.

"Delia was the one who called the police?" Jaxon asked.

"Yes," Landers said. "At that point, she didn't know

what Hank had done. She just wanted to get the kids some-place safe."

"But she allowed Hank to take the fall."

"She was scared. She called me and we talked," Director Landers explained.

Jaxon turned to the D.A. "They consulted you?"

"Yes," he admitted. "Delia didn't know what to do. She was going to turn herself in."

"But when we saw the crime pictures, the dozen stab wounds made by Hank, we realized he was dangerous," Landers added. "We thought it was best for Delia to con-tinue helping other kids and for Hank to be locked away."

As much as he hated to admit it, Jaxon understood their logic. But they had destroyed a kid's life. "Hank Tierney may have needed psychological help, but he was a teenager, and he deserved a chance," Jaxon said. "You ruined not just his life, but Avery's, as well."

"It was an impossible situation," Director Landers said.

Jaxon didn't intend to let him off the hook. "I understand you had client privilege," he said to the D.A. "But, Director Landers, you were sworn to uphold the law. Locking an in-nocent kid in jail was not the answer. Even worse, you knew there were extenuating circumstances, and you did nothing to help Hank's defense. And Joleen Mulligan should have been prosecuted herself."

"I know," Director Landers said. "There's not a day that's gone by that I haven't debated whether or not I did the right thing. But when I saw the rage inside that boy and those stab wounds, I honestly thought it was a matter of time be-fore he killed someone else. And Delia... She would never have survived prison."

"That wasn't your decision to make." Jaxon had to make this right. "The fact that all of you were willing to allow an innocent man to die to save your reputations is despicable." He reached for his phone.

He had to call a judge.

Then Avery.

Better yet, he wanted to give the director a chance to do the honorable thing. He gestured toward the phone. "Call the judge and tell the truth, Landers. If you don't turn yourself in, I'll arrest you myself."

Director Landers wiped at a bead of sweat trickling down his face. Snyderman nodded for Landers to make the call.

Jaxon stepped aside and punched Avery's number. She'd been upset when she'd left. Hopefully she'd driven straight home.

But Delia had been at her house before. What if she returned?

Fear needled him as he waited for Avery to answer. When she didn't, panic seized him, and he jogged outside to his SUV. If Delia suspected they were close to discovering the truth and that they might expose her, she might be desperate.

He had to find Avery.

AVERY STARED AT Delia Hanover in shock. "What are you doing, Delia?"

"You couldn't stop, couldn't let it alone, could you?" Delia cried.

"You were the one who threatened me over reopening the case." Confusion swirled in Avery's head. She was still reeling from learning that Jaxon had been working against her. And now Delia was holding a gun on her....

The woman's hand shook as she waved Avery to come in. "I tried to help you," Delia whispered. "I tried so hard, but I messed up."

Avery inhaled a deep breath. She had to stall. Figure out a way to convince Delia to drop the gun.

But Delia shoved the barrel into her ribs and pushed her into the den. Desperate for an escape, Avery glanced around the room. Basic furniture. A table loaded with folders. French doors leading to a patio...

A suitcase also stood by those doors, as if Delia had planned a trip.

If Delia planned to kill her and escape, Avery at least wanted answers.

"Why didn't you want me to reopen Hank's case?" Avery asked, although she had a bad feeling that she knew.

"I'm sorry about Hank, more than you'll ever know, Avery." Tears moistened Delia's troubled eyes. "I never meant for him to be arrested. It just...happened."

"What do you mean, it just happened?"

"I came over to see how you and Hank were doing, but then I heard you screaming and crying and saw Hank and Mulligan fighting. Then I watched him tie Hank to the bed."

Avery bit her lip as the memory washed over her. "You were the woman I heard that night. The one that whispered to me."

Delia nodded, a tear trickling down her cheek. "When I saw what he was doing, I panicked. I didn't know, not before then. I swear I didn't. But earlier that day, I found a note Erma Brant left."

"You should have removed us from the family then," Avery said sharply.

Delia began to pace, waving the gun with one hand and pulling at her hair with the other. "That's what I intended to do. That night, I drove over, planning to take you both away myself. But I saw Mulligan going in your room and you screamed, and I panicked. I grabbed a knife to protect myself, but when I tried to stop Mulligan, he came at me. He grabbed me and we fought, and I had the knife and...I stabbed him."

Avery could easily imagine the scenario she described. "You saved me," she whispered. "You cared enough to come and protect me," she said. "So why did you let Hank go to prison? You could have pleaded self-defense."

Delia's eyes flickered with wild panic as if she were reliving the night herself. "I was scared. It was my first job, and I wanted to make it work, wanted to help others. And my father... He's a judge. He warned me not to go into social work, said I wasn't cut out for it. I knew if I was arrested, it would not only ruin my career, but his, as well."

"You were worried about your career!" Avery said, her voice shrill. "What about my life? What about Hank's? He was just a kid and you stole his life from him."

A sob escaped Delia. "I didn't think he'd go to prison," she cried. "But when I saw how many times he stabbed Mulligan, I thought it was too late for Hank, that he was like his father, and he'd be better off locked away. I thought you'd be safer that way."

"Safer?" Avery cried. "Hank confessed to protect me. He's the only one who ever loved me, and because of me, and you—" she jabbed her finger in the air at Delia "—he's about to die."

Delia looked frantic, desperate. She paused by the window and rubbed her hand over her face, swiping at the tears. "I'm sorry, Avery. I'm so sorry. But—"

"There is no but," Avery said. "You can't let Hank die, Delia." She softened her voice, desperate to appeal to the woman's morals. "You're not a bad person. I know that. You care about the kids you help, just like you cared about us back then. A judge will understand that."

Delia shook her head back and forth, sobbing. "No, they won't. And my father... He'll hate me."

She raised the gun, and Avery held her breath, terrified Delia was going to shoot her.

But the woman turned the gun on herself and placed the barrel at her temple.

Chapter Twenty-Two

Jaxon checked the time as he drove from the jail. Delia would probably be at school. He punched the number for the office. "This is Texas Ranger Sergeant Ward. Is Delia Hanover at school today?"

"I'm afraid not. She called in sick."

"Where does she live?"

"I'm not supposed to give out that information."

"This is a police emergency. Lives may depend on it. Now give me her address."

The woman coughed nervously, then stuttered the address.

Jaxon recognized the street. Not far from the school.

He pressed the accelerator and sped down the road, rounding the curve on two wheels. Tires screeched, his adrenaline pumping as he neared the street. He veered right, slowing as he approached her house and saw Avery's car parked in front. He parked on the curb, slid from the vehicle and hurried toward the house, scanning the perimeter.

Early-morning sunlight slanted off the dry grass. The car in the neighboring driveway fired up its engine and the driver backed out, probably heading to work. A young mother across the street hustled her brood into a minivan. A jogger ran by with his chocolate Lab.

Everything looked normal and quiet. Just another day in Cherokee Crossing.

But instincts warned him that Delia Hanover might have figured out he and Avery were close to the truth, and that she was scared.

Her secret had been safely hidden for twenty years. She wouldn't want the truth to be exposed now.

He paused to listen as he reached the front door, but everything seemed quiet. Still, he pulled his gun at the ready, then stepped to the side and peered through the front window.

His chest clenched. Avery was standing within inches of Delia, while Delia clutched a gun in her hand.

He jumped back from the window so Delia wouldn't see him, then crept around the back of the house to sneak inside and surprise her from the rear.

But just as he reached the door, a gunshot blasted the air.

AVERY DIVED ON top of Delia, desperately trying to knock the gun from her hand. It went off, the bullet exploding in the ceiling, plaster raining down.

"Let me go!" Delia cried.

"You're not going to kill yourself," Avery shouted. "You're going to tell the truth and help free Hank."

Delia still had hold of the gun, and Avery struggled to pry it from her fingers. They rolled sideways, and she clawed at Delia's hand, trying to pin the woman down with her body.

But Delia was strong and used her weight to buck Avery off her. Avery fell to the floor, grasping for Delia's hand.

But Delia raised the gun again and kicked at Avery to keep her away.

Suddenly a crash sounded, and footsteps pounded.

Delia startled, and Avery crawled toward her to grab the gun. But Delia lifted her hand again, the gun wavering as she struggled to stand.

"Don't move, Delia. Put the weapon down!"

Jaxon burst into the room, his weapon aimed at Delia.

Delia cried out in surprise, and Avery scrambled backward away from the woman.

"Put it down," Jaxon ordered.

"I can't go to jail," Delia cried. "I can't…"

Jaxon cut his eyes toward Avery as if to ask if she was okay, and she gave him a quick nod.

"We'll explain what happened that night," Avery said in a low voice. "You defended yourself."

"But I let Hank be wrongly convicted," Delia cried. "I… should have told."

"Yes, you should have," Jaxon barked. "But it's not too late to do the right thing, Delia."

Delia was sobbing openly now, her hand shaking, the gun wavering toward Jaxon.

Feelings of betrayed splintered through Avery. Jaxon had kept his reason for investigating the case a secret to protect his boss.

But she didn't want him to die.

JAXON KEPT HIS hand steady as Delia backed up against the wall. "Delia, you don't want to shoot me or Avery. When you killed Mulligan, it was self-defense. You were trying to save two children from a monster. A judge and jury will sympathize with that." He lowered his voice. "But killing us is not the same thing. It's murder."

"I don't want to hurt either of you," Delia said, choking on more tears. "I just want this to be over."

"It will be when you lower the gun," Jaxon said. "We'll talk to the judge and explain."

But Delia shook her head back and forth, the panic on her face sending a chill through Jaxon.

"You've done good things for other children since that day," he said, grasping for a way to stop her from further self-destruction.

Delia blinked, her hand bobbing up and down. "But

it doesn't make up for that night." She glanced at Avery, sorrow wrenching her face. "I'm so sorry about Hank."

Then she swung the gun up toward her head.

Avery screamed, "No!"

Jaxon fired a shot at the floor beside Delia. She startled at the sound, and he lunged toward her and knocked the weapon from her hand.

The gun skittered to the floor, and he kicked it away. Then Delia doubled over into a knot on the floor and began to wail.

He glanced at Avery. "Are you okay?"

She nodded, although tears were streaming down her face, as well.

Delia was a pitiful mess, but she'd also tried to kill herself and taken Avery at gunpoint, so he yanked his handcuffs from his pocket, knelt and cuffed her.

She didn't fight him. Instead she crumbled, sobbing uncontrollably as he removed his phone and punched Deputy Kimball's number. "I'm bringing Delia Hanover in for the murder of Wade Mulligan. Ask a judge to meet us at the jail."

He went to Avery to help her up, but she waved his hands off and stood. Her breath was unsteady, pain still radiating from her eyes. "Can we get Hank out now?"

"That's the reason I asked the judge to meet us. He'll need to contact the governor and stop the execution. There will be a formal hearing, of course, and then hopefully Hank will be released."

A smile of relief curved Avery's mouth, but the sadness in her eyes remained.

She thought he'd betrayed her by withholding the truth about his initial reason for coming to Cherokee Crossing from her.

That secret had torn them apart and destroyed her trust in him.

And he didn't know how to win it back.

AVERY FELT NUMB as Jaxon escorted a sobbing Delia out to his SUV.

She followed them, her heart aching for Delia, yet she couldn't prevent the anger eating at her. Delia had deprived her brother of a life on the outside.

He was thirty-four now, not old, yet when he was freed, he'd have to start all over. He'd finished his GED in prison, but had no college or technical training. No job waiting or home or family.

Still, she couldn't wait to tell him that he was really going to be free.

Jaxon shut the back door, closing Delia in. She buried her head in her hands, doubling over as she cried.

"I'll call you when things are settled," Jaxon said.

"No, I'll follow you to the jail. I want to be there when Hank gets free."

"It won't happen today," Jaxon said. "It'll take time to set up the hearing."

"I know, but I want to see him," Avery said. "I have to let him know what's happened."

Jaxon hesitated. "Avery, go home and let me handle the arrangements. There's a lot to do. We have to book Delia, and I need to talk to the judge. And I haven't had time to tell you, but apparently Director Landers, my boss, knew what Delia did. He was a rookie back then, and he and Delia were dating. She told him what happened, but he covered it up. They both thought Hank was dangerous."

"That doesn't make it right."

"No, it doesn't," Jaxon said. "But we're going to."

His conviction warmed her. It must have been hard for him to admit that his boss had crossed the line. "Will you call and see if I can visit Hank and fill him in?"

Jaxon studied her for a long moment. "Of course. Hank deserves to know tonight."

His gaze locked with hers, and Avery's heart ached. Jaxon was the first man she'd ever really trusted.

And he'd let her down.

But in the end, he'd come through for her, and for her brother.

"I'm sorry about the director," he said, his jaw hard. "I didn't know, Avery. I swear I didn't."

She swallowed hard. She believed him. But her heart and her emotions were in shambles.

A sad look passed over his face; then he climbed into the SUV and started the engine.

Delia was still sobbing as he drove away.

Avery ignored the pang of sympathy tugging at her, jumped in her car and headed toward the prison.

Hank had waited twenty years for vindication.

She didn't want him to have to wait another minute.

AVERY LET HERSELF into her house, disappointment dogging her. She hadn't been able to see Hank.

Jaxon had phoned, but a brutal stabbing by another inmate had resulted in two dead guards and another dead inmate, and the prison was on twenty-four-hour lockdown.

Hank would have to go to bed tonight without knowing that he was going to be freed. She just prayed nothing happened to him until he was released.

But just to be on the safe side, she had phoned Ms. Ellis, the lawyer who'd initially been interested in Hank's case. The lawyer promised to contact Jaxon and to represent Hank in court. Avery's trust in the system was still shaky, and Avery felt better knowing she and Hank had another professional on their side.

Avery hesitated as she entered, remembering the pictures Delia had cut up and left on her bed. Remembering the words she'd written and that threatening phone call.

Delia had obviously been terrified of the truth being exposed.

Shaken by the day's events, she showered and pulled on her pajamas, then poured herself a glass of wine and padded outside to her screened porch. She settled in the swing, pushing it back and forth with her foot as she sipped the wine.

Outside the wind tossed dead leaves around, and the trees swayed, the woods dark and desolate looking. She'd been afraid of the dark half her life.

She'd been afraid of so many things.

Afraid of getting close to anyone. Of letting a man touch her.

Just as she was afraid of owning her house. Of having a pet. It hurt too much to lose them.

Jaxon had changed all that. And he hadn't abandoned the case, even though his boss had turned out to be dirty.

She closed her eyes and remembered his fingers roving over her body, his tongue touching her intimate places, his body coupling with hers, and heat suffused her.

She had practically begged Jaxon to make love to her.

And he had been gentle. Loving.

He'd even promised to stop if she'd wanted him to.

How could she blame him for having sex with her when she'd wanted him so badly?

When she still did?

A lonely feeling washed over her as she studied the night sky.

Jaxon had never mentioned love or wanting a relationship. When the case was dismissed and Hank was set free, she would need to help Hank get on his feet and figure out what to do with his life. With his second chance.

Jaxon would move on to another case.

And she would have to let him.

Chapter Twenty-Three

"Hank Tierney, you are hereby exonerated of the murder conviction against you for the death of Wade Mulligan." The judge angled himself toward Hank. "It is a travesty that it took so long for justice to be served, but you do realize the part you played in impeding the investigation?"

Hank sat stoically, his face etched in disbelief. "Yes, sir."

"That said, the court apologizes for the injustice done to you by the system and the failure of your attorney at the time to provide an adequate defense. In addition, the officer in charge of the investigation has admitted to omitting key evidence in the crime and faces charges himself.

"In the light of new evidence, you are free to go."

He pounded the gavel, and everyone except Hank stood. He was still sitting in shock by Jaxon and Ms. Ellis, who patted him on the back. "Congratulations, Hank, you've been exonerated. Your name is clear now. And I'll see what I can do about obtaining monetary restitution."

Avery jumped up and hurried around to her brother. "Hank, did you hear, you're free?"

Her brother slowly looked up at her, tears pooling in his eyes. "For real?"

"Yes, for real," Avery said with a nervous laugh. "I tried to see you last night at the prison to give you a heads-up, but the prison was on lockdown and they wouldn't let me visit."

Hank looked at Jaxon, then the lawyer, then her. "Delia, our social worker, killed that bastard Mulligan?"

"Yes." Avery drew him into a hug. "It's over, Hank. It's finally over and you can go home."

"I don't believe it," Hank mumbled.

She pulled away, and Jaxon extended his hand to Hank. "Believe it, Hank. It was too long in coming, but justice finally prevailed."

And not a minute too soon. Two more days and Hank would have been put to death.

A smile started on Hank's face, and he shook Jaxon's hand. But his frown returned when he faced Avery. "You said I can go home. But I don't have a home or a job or anywhere to go."

Avery's heart swelled. "Yes, you do—you're coming home with me. I'm even thinking of buying my little house."

He looked at her with such relief that she hugged him again. "I know it'll take time, brother, but we'll work it out. The important thing is that you were exonerated. You're not only free, but your name has been cleared."

Not that it would replace the twenty years he'd lost.

Hank turned to Jaxon with a sheepish look. "Thank you, Sergeant Ward. I never trusted a cop before, but I appreciate what you did."

Avery's gaze met Jaxon's, but he simply shrugged. "I was just doing my job."

So that was it, Avery thought. He had just been doing his job. Nothing personal.

She should be so detached.

Her father appeared then, cutting off any further exchange. He looked old and weathered, but he had tried to do the right thing for Hank at his own expense.

Maybe it was time for forgiveness.

"Thank you, Dad," Avery said. "Hank and I appreciate what you did for him."

Hank rubbed a hand over his shaved head, his expression torn. "Yeah, thanks. I...never would have expected you to do something like that."

Their father gave a self-deprecating laugh. "To tell you the truth, neither did I. But when I saw the news and thought about you dying when it was my fault you and your sister ended up with that family, I had to do something."

Hank hesitated, but shook his father's hand. Avery bit her lip to keep from crying.

Maybe she could put her family back together again.

The thought gave her hope, but Jaxon turned and headed out the door, and a dull ache rippled through her.

Only Jaxon wouldn't be part of her future.

THE PAST TWENTY-FOUR hours had been hell. Jaxon hated that he'd been forced to make the director turn himself in. Everyone in the Texas Ranger Division was upset, and Landers was right—already the hounds were surfacing to question his other arrests.

Snyderman received sanctions, but the moment Landers had confided in him, hiring Snyderman as his attorney, client privilege kicked in.

Delia's father had shown up, irate, and accused Jaxon of framing Delia, but the woman had confessed.

Now he watched Avery leave with her brother and father, grateful at last that she could have the family she deserved.

But as he walked outside to his vehicle, a sense of loss engulfed him. And when he made it to his ranch, the place he loved, the vast wide-open spaces and sprawling land suddenly looked empty and lonely.

Just like Avery, he'd guarded his heart all his life. Had allowed himself only a physical connection with a woman. Had focused on his job.

Because catching killers was a lot less scary than sharing your heart.

He climbed out, his boots crunching as he walked across the pasture to the barn. He hadn't spent much time here lately. Things were looking run-down.

He needed help.

An idea struck him, and he returned to his SUV and headed back toward town.

Avery might not forgive him for Director Landers, but maybe he could make amends by offering her brother a job on his ranch.

It wouldn't be easy for Hank to acclimate back into society. And if Hank didn't want the job, that was fine.

But Jaxon wanted to give the man a second chance.

Then maybe Avery would give him a second chance, as well.

AVERY HAD JUST walked outside to plant some bulbs when Jaxon pulled up. She'd left Hank inside with Ms. Ellis—Lisa—giving them some privacy. Apparently something had sparked between them when they met, and Avery thought her brother might just have a lover in his future.

But the moment Avery saw Jaxon, nerves fluttered in her stomach. What if something had gone wrong and he was here to take Hank back to prison?

When he climbed from the driver's side, tingles of desire danced down her spine, and she drank in his strong masculine presence.

She'd never met a man like him. She'd certainly never meet another.

"Jaxon," she said, grappling for words. "Is everything all right? The judge. Hank—"

"Everything is fine. Don't worry, your brother is free and clear."

Relief made her sag against the shovel she was holding.

"You're planting flowers?" Jaxon asked.

She nodded. "Hank has missed the seasons," she said. "I want him to see the tulips come to life in the spring."

"Nice."

For a moment, they stood looking at each other, an awkward silence lingering between them. Finally he tipped his Stetson.

"I stopped by because of Hank. Him and your father."

Avery's stomach knotted again. "Why? What's wrong?"

"Nothing." He threaded his fingers through his hair, then settled his hat back in place. "When you were at the ranch, I told you I'm busy, gone on cases, and need some help working the horses, repairing fences. If your father and brother want a job and don't mind hard work, I could use them on the spread."

Avery leaned the shovel against the side of the house. "You're serious, Jaxon?"

"Yes."

"That would be perfect. I know Hank would like to work outdoors." She hesitated. "But are you sure you want to take my father on? He is an ex-con."

"He redeemed himself at the end," Jaxon said. "Everyone deserves a second chance."

Love bloomed in Avery's chest. Was he asking for one? "You are an amazing man, Jaxon."

He shrugged. "It's the least I can do."

"You've already done enough. My goodness, you tracked down Delia and saved Hank."

"When I pulled up at the house and heard gunfire last night, I thought I'd lost you," Jaxon said in a gruff voice.

Avery licked her lips, touched. "I jumped Delia to keep her from committing suicide."

"That's even more admirable," Jaxon said. "Especially considering the fact that she was responsible for Hank's incarceration and partially responsible for your abuse by leaving you in that devil's home."

Avery softened at his possessive tone.

"I know it was difficult for you," she said in a low murmur. "That you were in a tough spot with your boss."

Jaxon shrugged, his rugged face set in a frown. But his eyes locked with hers, and something heady flickered there.

Need? Desire? Passion?

"You did it for me, didn't you?" Avery whispered.

"Partly. And partly for your brother." His voice cracked, and he reached for her. Circled his arms around her wrist and drew her to him. "But I did it mostly because it was the right thing to do. I couldn't have lived with myself if I'd covered up the truth."

"Well, whatever your reason, I appreciate it." She thumbed a strand of his dark hair from his forehead, and her finger tingled. She wanted to touch him all over again.

His eyes flared with hunger. "I'm not here for your thanks."

She smiled at the glint in his eyes. "Why are you here, then?"

A heartbeat passed. His thick arousal pressed against her belly. Her heart drummed so loud she could hear it roaring in her ears.

She ached to have him closer.

"I came for this." He whispered her name in a husky tone that made her shiver all over, then pressed his lips to hers. Erotic sensations mingled with emotions, nearly overpowering her, and she kissed him back, tangling her tongue with his in a frenzy of wild abandon.

When he finally pulled away, they were both breathless, but he held her close and nuzzled her neck with his lips. "I love you, Avery."

Avery's heart fluttered. All her hopes and dreams had been stirred to life the past few days with Jaxon.

Could she dare believe that they would come true?

With this man, maybe she could.

She was tired of running and being scared.

He seemed to be searching her face, and she realized that he was scared, too. Maybe nervous that she didn't return his feelings.

Empowered by that thought, she looped her arms around his neck, then brushed herself against him in a slow seductive move. "I love you, too, Jaxon. I never thought I could... love any man. But I love you with all my heart."

He teased her lips apart with his tongue. "Good. 'Cause I don't want to be alone anymore. And that ranch is awful lonely without you."

"Really?" she said in a teasing voice.

"I can still smell you on my sheets." He rubbed his forehead against hers. "And my shower is big enough for two."

"I noticed."

"You're going to buy this house, though?"

She shrugged. "I just wanted to finally have a permanent home. Maybe get a dog."

A smile twitched at his eyes. "A ranch is a great place for a dog."

"I bet it is."

Passion glazed his eyes. "I want you in my bed, Avery. But that's not all." His voice broke. "I want you to be my wife."

Her heart soared as he swung her up in his arms and carried her to his SUV. Ten minutes later, they parked at his ranch.

She climbed out, breathing in the pure beauty of the land and the man—and the fact that he wanted to share his life with her.

He swept her up in his arms again, kissed her with all the fervor of a lover desperate for more, then carried her inside to bed.

They made love all through the night, whispering promises that they would be together the rest of their lives.

Promises she knew that the man in her arms would keep.

* * * * *

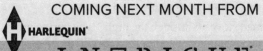

REQUEST YOUR FREE BOOKS!
2 FREE NOVELS PLUS 2 FREE GIFTS!

❤ HARLEQUIN

INTRIGUE

BREATHTAKING ROMANTIC SUSPENSE

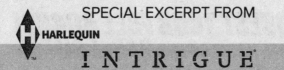
"The woman in Greenleaf Bar was you?"

"You don't remember?"

"Vaguely."

He struggled to put things in perspective. That had been a hell of a night. He'd stopped at the first bar he'd come to after leaving the rodeo. A blonde had sat down next to him. As best he remembered, he'd given her an earful about the rodeo, life and death as he'd become more and more inebriated.

She must have offered him a ride back to his hotel since his truck had still been at the bar when he'd gone looking for it the next morning. If Brit was telling the truth, the woman must have gone into the motel with him and they'd ended up doing the deed.

If so, he'd been a total jerk. She'd been as drunk as him and driven or she'd willingly taken a huge risk.

Hard to imagine the woman staring at him now ever

being that careless or impulsive.

"Is that your normal pattern, Mr. Dalton?" Brit asked. "Use a woman to satisfy your physical needs and then ride off to the next rodeo?"

"That's a little like the armadillo calling the squirrel roadkill, isn't it? I'm sure I didn't coerce you into my bed if I was so drunk I can't remember the experience."

"I can assure you that you're nowhere near that irresistible. I have never been in your bed."

"Whew. That's a relief. I'd have probably died of frostbite."

"This isn't a joking matter."

"I'm well aware. But I'm not the enemy here, so you can quit talking to me like I just climbed out from under a slimy rock. If you're not Kimmie's mother, who is?"

"My twin sister, Sylvie Hamm."

Twin sisters. That explained Brit's attitude. Probably considered her sister a victim of the drunken sex urges he didn't remember. It also explained why Brit Garner looked familiar.

"So why is it I'm not having this conversation with Sylvie?"

"She's dead."

Find out what happens next in
MIDNIGHT RIDER
by Joanna Wayne,
available January 2015 wherever
Harlequin Intrigue® books and ebooks are sold.

"We've got to get you out of here."

"I am not helpless, Pete. I've been in self-defense courses my entire life. And I know how to shoot. My gun's in the bag we left outside."

Good to know, but he wasn't letting her near that bag. He dropped the key ring on the floor near her hands. "Find one that looks like it's to a regular inside door. Like a broom closet. I'm going to lock you inside."

"Are you sure they're still out there?"

"The chopper's on the ground. The blades are still rotating. No telling how many were already here ready to ambush us." He watched two shadows cross the patio. "Let's move. Next to the snack bar, there's a maintenance door. Run. I'll lay down cover if we need it."

They ran. He could see the shadows but no one followed. Hopefully they didn't have eyes on him or Andrea. He heard the keys and a couple of curses behind him, then a door swung open enough for his charge to squeeze through.

He saw the glint of sun off a mirror outside. They were watching.

"Can you lock the door? Will it lock without the key?"

"I think so."

"Keep the keys with you. I don't need them. Less risky." Bullets could work as a key to unlock, but they might not risk injuring Andrea. He was counting on that.

"But, Pete—"

"Let me do my job, Andrea. Once you're inside, see if you can get into the crawl space. They just saw you open the door. Hide till the cavalry arrives."

"You mean the navy. He won't let us down," she said from the other side of the door. "This is his thing, after all."

Pete had done all he could do to hide her. Now he needed to protect her.

Find out what happens next in
THE SHERIFF
by Angi Morgan,
available January 2015 wherever
Harlequin Intrigue® books and ebooks are sold.